William Hurrell Mallock

The Old Order Changes

A novel. Part 3

William Hurrell Mallock

The Old Order Changes
A novel. Part 3

ISBN/EAN: 9783337051143

Printed in Europe, USA, Canada, Australia, Japan

Cover: Foto ©Andreas Hilbeck / pixelio.de

More available books at **www.hansebooks.com**

THE OLD ORDER CHANGES

A Novel

BY

W. H. MALLOCK

AUTHOR OF 'IS LIFE WORTH LIVING?' 'SOCIAL EQUALITY' ETC.

'Cette importune économie politique se glisse partout et se mêle
à tout, et je crois vraiment que c'est elle qui a dit, *nihil humani a
me alienum puto*'—BASTIAT

IN THREE VOLUMES

VOL. II.

LONDON

RICHARD BENTLEY & SON, NEW BURLINGTON STREET

Publishers in Ordinary to Her Majesty the Queen

1886

B

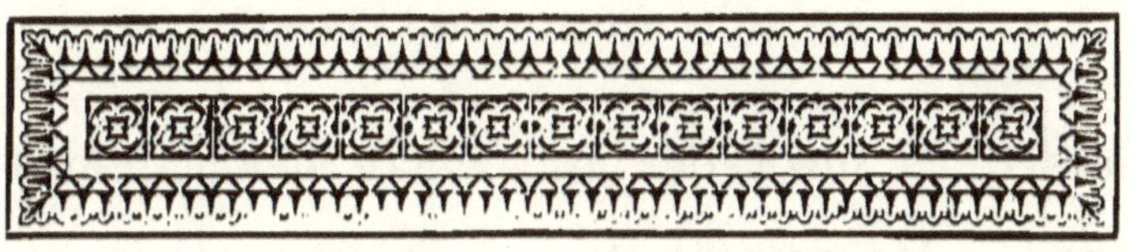

CHAPTER VIII.

MRS. HARLEY proved eventually to have been not far wrong in her anticipations ; though there was one dreadful moment which made her fear she had been so. This was the moment of Foreman's introduction to Lady Mangotsfield. The great lady, as soon as he was brought up to her, raised her wrinkled eyelids with a mild benignity, and was inclining her head very slightly but encouragingly, in recognition of Lord B——'s political foundling, when the foundling, to her astonishment, had actually the presumption to say that 'he was very much pleased to meet her and make her acquaintance.'   He said it, too, in a voice that had actually the presumption to be genial ; and he filled up the measure of his audacity by unhesitatingly holding out his hand to her.

Lady Mangotsfield gave as good a start as she had done on the previous evening at the mention of Mr. Snapper ; and raising her eyeglass as her greeting died on her lips, she scrutinized Foreman from head to foot, wondering, so it seemed, if he could really be the person she had heard about. At last she said, very much in the same tone she might have used when engaging a servant bringing a doubtful character : ' You used, I think, to know Lord B——, didn't you ? '

' Oh, yes,' said Foreman, perfectly unabashed. ' I used at one time to have many conversations with him.'

' And is it true,' she went on, ' that he wanted to put you into Parliament ? '

It was now Foreman's turn to start, and Mrs. Harley, who was watching him, said afterwards that at this question his very beard was beginning to bristle. Luckily, however, before he had time to answer, dinner was announced, and his arm was claimed by Mrs. Harley, Lady Mangotsfield being carried off by Carew.

At dinner things were on a securer footing. Foreman was placed in very excellent custody. Mr. Stanley was on one side of him, and Mrs. Harley on the other ; whilst Carew divided Mrs. Harley from Lady Mangotsfield. Foreman in this position was almost powerless for mischief, and his conversation became little more than a tap which those near him could turn on and off as they chose. Mrs. Harley felt now quite in her element, and everything went exactly as she designed it. 'I forget, Lady Mangotsfield,' she began, ' if you are an admirer of Thackeray ? We were talking of him just before dinner, and we were having a grand dispute about him.'

'There's nobody like him now, my dear,' said Lady Mangotsfield; 'not so clever, I mean. When his books came out I read them—so we all of us did. But I didn't like them. There was always a vulgar tone in them. What does Lord Aiden say?'

'I,' Lord Aiden replied, 'say exactly the same thing; except that I think I should put it in stronger language. You, Mr. Foreman, hold also the same opinion?'

Lady Mangotsfield again put up her eye-glass and looked at Foreman, as if in bewilderment as to what a man like that should know about such a subject. Mrs. Harley meanwhile was joining issue with all of them.

'I confess,' she was saying, 'I can't see what you mean. You call Thackeray vulgar. Why, he was always lashing vulgarity.'

'If he was,' exclaimed Foreman, breaking

out into a chuckling laugh, 'if he was, he was like Job, scraping his own sores.'

Lady Mangotsfield dropped her eyeglass. She looked more surprised than ever; but the surprise changed its character. Her withered lips worked themselves into a smile, and leaning a little forwards, with a voice of tremulous approbation, 'That's very coarse, Mr. Foreman,' she said, 'but it's very true—very true indeed.'

'Mr. Foreman, however,' said Lord Aiden, 'thinks one thing which I confess I don't understand. He thinks that Thackeray was our chief political novelist.'

'Oh, no,' said Lady Mangotsfield, shaking her head as if that answered the question, 'oh, no; poor dear Lord B—— was that. No political novels were ever written like his.'

'Excuse me,' said Foreman, 'but Thackeray exhibited what Lord B—— hardly tried to describe, and that is the origin of the modern Radical party—the party which calls itself the party of the working-men and of the people.'

'In Thackeray's days,' said Lady Mangotsfield, ' there was no such a party existing. We were all very good to the poor, but nobody cared anything about the people. Politicians in those days were gentlemen.'

'Do you think the Radical party,' said Foreman, ' cares anything about the people now—or about the poor either? Not they. I've watched them for twenty years, and the one idea in their minds——' He paused and looked round the table to see if he was being listened to. He was. There was silence, and then he resumed his sentence. ' The one idea in their minds is precisely the same idea that occupies Thackeray's mind through every one of his novels.'

' And pray,' said Lady Chislehurst, ' what idea is that ? '

'The uneasy and envious inferiority of a *bourgeoisie* in contact with an aristocracy,' said Foreman, in a voice so emphatic that it seemed to defy dissent. 'Every virtue and every vice is measured in his mind by its relation to that : and this essentially limited and middle-class source of temptation is for him the supreme evil that man has to struggle with.'

'Perfectly true,' said Lord Aiden. 'No criticism could be truer.'

'I,' said Mrs. Harley, ' can't admit that for a moment. Of Thackeray's own character we are of course none of us talking : we are talking of the class which Mr. Foreman says is analyzed by him, and I quite deny that either in Thackeray's books or in reality their lives as a rule are filled by this one idea he speaks of. I have known—I know—many number of the unmistakable middle-class myself——'

'My dear,' interposed Lady Mangotsfield,

'I'm sure you know a number of shocking people.'

'And I can only say,' Mrs. Harley continued, 'that simpler people, people more unworldly, and less pushing I never met with in my life.'

'You misunderstand me,' said Foreman. 'Two-thirds of the middle-class are Conservative. You may take their content. I willingly make you a present of it. I am talking only of the one-third, which is Radical, and that one-third represents human nature for Thackeray. According to Thackeray man has only two temptations—to fawn on his superiors, or else to spit in their faces. Had he not shown us with all the force of his genius that there are men of whom this is really true, it would for many of us be very difficult to believe it. But there are such men—there is a whole class of them ; and the Radicalism of to-day is the expression of their corporate character. In Thackeray's days, Lady Mangotsfield, they had not learnt how to express it. Will you allow me to tell you out of my own humble life a little anecdote which will help to explain my meaning? In the country town where I used to live when a boy, the great lady was the doctor's wife, Mrs. Hopkins, and Dr. Hopkins had no more admiring patient than Mrs. Skinner, the wife of the wealthiest draper. Well, one Christmas Mrs. Hopkins gave two memorable parties: the first for her best friends, the second for her second best. Mrs. Skinner—I remember the event now—poor soul, she was asked to the second; and she met the wife of the butcher, and was given a stale mince-pie. From that day forth the doctor, once so infallible, became, according to her, an ignorant brazen quack, and she threatened to go to law with him for having sent her the wrong prescription. Now, in place of the Hopkinses put the gentlemen

of the country. Take the condition of good
Mrs. Skinner's mind, give it political instead
of private libel to work with; and there you
have a complete and accurate image of our
Radical leaders when they pretend to a popular
policy. Snapper, for instance, after a public
meeting—a public meeting at which he has
been denouncing the landlords, were there
only some talisman that could force his real
thoughts from him, no fun since the world
began could equal it! Bless my soul, with
him and with all his followers, the real
grievance is that they cannot dine with dukes,
not that millions of wage-slaves can get no
dinners at all.'

' Perfectly true,' said Lady Mangotsfield
to Carew, ' I never heard anything truer; if
only the dear man would make a little less
noise about it.'

' You don't think, then, Mr. Foreman,'
said Lady Chislehurst, who was at heart some-

thing of a reformer, ' that these Radicals really care about doing any good to the people—about removing any of their grievances ?'

'I hope,' said Foreman, 'you won't think that the Devil is quoting Scripture when I answer "By their works you shall know them." Find me any measure characteristically Radical, or supported by the Radicals with anything like enthusiasm, which is not remarkable for these two things : its imbecile puerility as directed to the assistance of the people, and its malevolent ingenuity as directed to the humbling of the landed aristocracy. In that last point alone is the Radical party consistent. As for their leaders—bless my soul!—I run them over in my own mind, and they are all as like as one pea to another—every man jack of them. Each one of them, with his little hoard of personal bitterness, carries the scowl of the baffled or hopeless toady under the pasteboard mask of the vapid smirking philanthropist. The desire of a Mr. Japhet Snapper to rob the gentlemen of their position is simply a fermentation of his desire to lick their shoes.'

' Mr. Foreman,' said Mrs. Harley, ' since when have you become so exclusive ? '

Foreman stared at her. ' I can't imagine what you mean,' he said.

' I am thinking,' said Mrs. Harley, ' of the magnificent way in which you contrast Mr. Snapper with the *gentlemen* of the country, who seem according to you to be synonymous with the country gentleman.'

' They are so,' said Foreman, squaring his elbows and leaning on them, ' the country gentlemen and their families. I am quite aware that to many this use of the word is offensive, for to many people there is nothing so offensive as truth. But a gentleman is a man who is born in a certain way ; he is the same thing as a *gentilhomme*, and any other definition, as Dr. Johnson says, is fantastic. I am myself not a gentleman any more than I am a negro. By birth I belong to the middle-classes, and, thanks to my opinions, I belong to no class at all.'

' Really, Mr. Foreman,' began Lady Chislehurst, ' a man of your intellect and education——' But Foreman politely interrupted her.

' Excuse me,' he said, ' I know what you would tell me exactly. You would tell me that I was a gentleman because I was a man of education, and in one sense you would speak sincerely. But would you say the same, I should like to know, if I wished to marry your daughter?'

Had such a question been asked with any trace of personal feeling, it would naturally have produced the most awkward situation imaginable. But Foreman smiled as he spoke with the most perfect and most phlegmatic apathy, and though Lady Chislehurst coloured at the first moment, a glance at his face at once made her calm again. As for Lady Mangotsfield, she needed no calming whatever.

'A nice unassuming person, this friend of yours,' she said to Carew, and then turning her glasses on Foreman with a twinkle of condescending encouragement, ' If everyone else,' she said, 'were like you, Mr. Foreman, England would not long be in the state it is at present.'

' By God!' roared Foreman, ' you are perfectly right there.'

Lady Mangotsfield's last sentence had been too much for him. Everybody stared at him thunderstruck—everybody but Lady Mangotsfield herself. As for her, she merely turned to Carew, and wrinkling her forehead, as if the sound had pained her, ' It's a pity,' she said, ' that in his manners he's not a little more what one could wish him. But on the whole I like him. He speaks the truth, and he don't pretend to be a gentleman.'

'Yes,' said Lord Aiden to Foreman, as they were strolling into the drawing-room, laying his hand as he spoke on the other's shoulder, 'I always thought myself this social envy of the landlords was really at the bottom of the popular philanthropy of the Radicals.'

'Well,' said Foreman, with a grim though good-natured smile, 'we Socialists shall cure them of that at least, for we shall by-and-by leave the landlords very little to envy.'

CHAPTER IX.

F Lady Mangotsfield liked Foreman during dinner, her liking did not prove to be a very durable feeling, though, to do her justice, it only departed gradually. They had hardly been in the drawing-room five minutes before he had returned of his own accord to the subject which the others, for his sake, would have studiously avoided.

' We were talking at dinner,' Lady Chislehurst,' he began, ' about gentlemen and not gentlemen. I am told that the other night you had *Le Bourgeois Gentilhomme* acted here.

Do you remember what Cléonte says to Monsieur Jourdain : *Je vous dirai franchement que je ne suis point gentilhomme.* If only our *bourgeoisie* had the same common sense in England ! As for me, my own parentage was this : my father was a small grocer, my mother was the daughter of a parson. She married against the will of her family ; in your class you would say she made a *mésalliance.* The parson's father was an auctioneer, and from him, at his son's death, there descended to my mother some fifteen thousand pounds—enough to maintain, and it did maintain, a family, in that swinish comfort which the middle classes adore, and which tends to foster a viler type of life than anything does, except the lowest stage of privation.'

'Well,' said Lady Mangotsfield to Lord Aiden, as if making the best of things, ' he's quite right not to be ashamed of his parents, though he needn't think we're so anxious to hear all about his private affairs.'

' I don't want,' Foreman was meanwhile proceeding, unconsciously anticipating this criticism, ' I don't want to trouble you with my own biography ; I only want to show you this—from what position I look out upon the world, and how perfectly free I am from aristocratic bias when I criticise, as I have done, the middle-class Radical party. I have left my own class, but I have not tried to enter yours, except as a curious observer. That I have done, and in so impartial a spirit that I could, if I liked, give my own impressions of you with as little prejudice as if you were South Sea Islanders.'

A slight cloud was gathering on Lady Mangotsfield's face. Lady Chislehurst's, on the contrary, was brightening with the sunlight of inquiry. ' Well,' she said, ' give us some of your impressions—do! We are all listening.

Nothing could interest us more. I feel,' she added, as she smoothed down her rustling silk, 'just as if one was going to hear one's character told from one's hand.'

'You want to know,' said Foreman, looking round him, ' what I, an outsider, think of you. I'm very blunt; I go to the point at once. I think, then, that you, the ladies and the gentlemen of England, are the only people who behave like ladies and gentlemen ; for all such behaviour is based upon one thing—a sense of inherited and unworked for superiority. Other classes, no doubt, may try to copy it, but they have not the sense I speak of, so the copy is merely a sham. It is as meaningless as a portcullis would be at the gate of a Clapham villa.'

' Come,' interposed Mrs. Harley, ' I shall make a stand now in earnest. If you are going to talk again about what classes are vulgar and not vulgar, I must at any rate tell you this. I've met with more vulgarity and more snobbishness in the very highest sections of society than I ever have done in any other. And as for refinement, cultivation, and real consideration for others, I could show you these in every grade of the middle classes—yes, and amongst the workmen too.'

' My dear Mrs. Harley,' said Lord Aiden, ' that I can well believe. A snob is simply a person, no matter what his station, who judges aristocratic society by the standards and with the feelings of the middle class: and many fine people, now classes are so jostled together, have learnt to do this, as we all of us here must know. Snobbishness is a thing quite distinct from worldliness. It is simply an ignorant and distorted social judgment, which only becomes offensive, indeed it only becomes apparent, when snobs who are worldly act upon it.'

' There's more truth,' exclaimed Foreman,

'in what you have just said, than perhaps your Lordship appreciates. Those qualities, Mrs. Harley, which you just now named to us—they make a man better than a gentleman, but they don't make him a gentleman, and I can't think why you should try to prove they do.'

'Dear Lady Mangotsfield,' said Lady Chislehurst, 'and what is your view of the matter?'

'What, my dear? What?' said Lady Mangotsfield sharply. 'I've not been listening to what has been said lately. I don't at all understand what it all is you have been talking about.' This reply was accompanied by a slight rustling sound; and the party then perceived that Lady Mangotsfield had a newspaper in front of her, and either was, or was at least pretending to be, quite uncon- scious of the conversation. It was all very well, she thought, that Foreman should admit he was not a gentleman, and should expose the malcontents of his own rank in life with the authority that comes of near acquaintance-ship. It might even be borne—though this was perhaps a liberty—that he should compliment gentlemen on the superiority of their breeding. But that he should presume to go into such niceties as what good breeding was, and that her friends should be discussing with him—the son of a small grocer—the most delicate social problems that occupy high society—this was more than Lady Mangots-field could endure. A copy of the 'Figaro' had happened to be beside her, which afforded her the means of making a silent protest; and though it is true she was holding it upside down, she managed to fix her eyes on it with an air of severe abstraction.

'We've been talking,' said Lady Chisle-hurst, 'about the difference between snobs and gentlemen. We thought it was a subject in which you took a good deal of interest.'

'Not I, my dear,' said Lady Mangotsfield. 'I don't know anything about snobs. In my day we used to have nothing to do with them. Mr. Carew, may I ask you to light me a candle and ring for my servant. I think I will go upstairs now. I shall have a great deal,' she added as she was going out of the door, 'I shall have a great deal to tell that fine gentleman Mr. Inigo, if I see him. He, I've no doubt, will be charmed to hear all about it.'

It was well for Lady Mangotsfield's feelings that she left the scene when she did, for Foreman, despite her inattention, was fast warming with his subject, and all the others were anxious to keep him going. Hardly had Lady Mangotsfield had the door closed upon her, when he had again fastened on Mrs. Harley and caught up the thread of his argument.

' Why, Mrs. Harley,' he said, ' should you be so anxious to prove all your virtuous friends gentlemen ? And why, Lady Chislehurst, should you be shy of denying the title to me ? The distinction really is hardly worth fighting for. You and your friends will possess it a little longer, but nobody will possess it for long. When it goes it will be a pretty thing lost ; but it is merely a pretty thing now, though once it was much more.'

' And why ? said Lady Chislehurst, ' do you think it need go at all ? '

' And why, pray,' said Mrs. Harley, ' should it not be shared by everybody ? '

' Why?' echoed Foreman. ' For a precious simple reason. Because you can never turn everybody into a small and exceptional class. That is why you can't confer it on others. Before very long you will have ceased to be exceptional ; and this is why you will soon lose it yourselves. How do you differ from the wealthy middle classes ? In this—that along with your wealth you have traditions of hereditary power and usefulness. Well, your part is played ; you are useful and powerful no longer. Don't think I speak from any ill-feeling against an aristocracy as such. As a Socialist—I suppose, Mrs. Harley, I may use that terrible word now—as a Socialist, I regard you as the survival of a class that was once both noble and necessary : whereas the modern middle class, the slave-driving *bourgeoisie*, has been bad from the very beginning, and every day it is growing worse.'

'Do you think,' said Carew, 'that, supposing we made an effort, there would be a chance for us still of retrieving a lost position?'

'No,' said Foreman bluffly; 'I don't think, Mr. Carew, that there would ; and if you like it, I'll tell you why, though Lord Aiden—he may not know it—has really told you already.

You, the gentlemen of the country, the old landed families — I include, too, the newer ones which have acquired the good-will of their predecessors—you no longer stand on your own proper foundations. You are reduced financially to mere hangers-on of the *bourgeoisie*. Your material splendour, which once had a real meaning, is still, no doubt, maintained. But how ? Here is an instance. Some while since I went from curiosity to see the castle of a certain duke. During the last ten years it has been what he calls restored. The yellow stucco of ninety years ago has given place to the towers of a Gothic castle. Well, what does this imposing transformation mean ? That his Grace has become more powerful as a territorial noble ? Not a bit of it. What it means is this : that he has five million dollars' worth of railway stock in America. Such is the case with the whole body of the aristocracy.'

'I wish,' murmured Lord Aiden to Carew, 'I could say it was the case with me.'

'It is a type,' went on Foreman, 'of the present position of you all. You could no longer live like seigneurs if you were not half tradesmen.'

'But surely,' said Mrs. Harley, 'these are the very people—these rich landlords with capital to fall back upon—who as landlords can be most generous to their tenantry.'

'Yes,' said Foreman, 'and some of them are generous. Some of them have returned 50 per cent. of their rents, where 10 per cent. would have been more than ample. Such generosity does more harm than good; and, apart from that, you seem quite to forget the operatives—the hands, as you call them, the poor jaded underfed wage-slaves, drudging somewhere in the foul air of some factory, who really supply the cost of it. You quite forget, or you else have not yet learnt the one grand truth that we Socialists mean to teach you. The profits of capital are the spoliation of labour; and it is as impossible for a capitalist to be a real friend of the people as for the owner of a gin-palace to be a real apostle of temperance.'

Foreman's savage accent was in this last utterance; and Mrs. Harley, who knew it well, detected its presence not without anxiety. Mr. Stanley, however, seemed perfectly un-ruffled; and with an air of authority which seemed to surprise Foreman said, 'There you raise two quite distinct points. Allow me for the present to put the last one aside—the illegitimacy of the profits derived from capi-tal; and accepting them as a fact, I will put one question to you. You admit that our aristocracy still has a tradition of leadership. Don't you think that an aristocrat who re-ceives the profits of capital may possibly administer them in the old aristocratic spirit. For, after all, what are they ? Merely a new form of power.'

'Ah,' said Foreman, with a slightly malicious laugh, 'I am coming to that now. For the moment, if you like, I will grant that your profits are right enough. I will keep that crow to pick with you by-and-by : and since you wish it, I will answer you this first. Only I tell you again, Lord Aiden has anticipated me in what just now he said about snobs and snobbishness.'

'What did I say ? I forget,' murmured Lord Aiden languidly.

'You said, my lord,' said Foreman, 'that a number of fine people had learnt to judge of one another by the standards of the class below them. And that is what I have to say in answer to Mr. Stanley. Not only has our aristocracy cast in its lot with the *bourgeoisie* financially, but it has become corrupted by

the ideas of the *bourgeoisie* socially.   You
have often told me, Mrs. Harley, and I have
gathered it myself from the papers, that if
some Manchester slave-driver wants to succeed in London, thousands of pounds are
spent on a single ball, and to this, with the
aid of some fashionable lady as an accomplice,
the fashionable world comes flocking like so
many moths about a candle.'

'Yes,' said Harley, 'that is perfectly true ;
and next week they will have forgotten the
host and hostess.'

'I think, dear,' said his wife, 'that you
are wrong there.   They will be quite civil
to them ; and will ask them, in return, to
their own balls.   But the civility will be so
distant that virtually it amounts to an insult;
and my only wonder is that these people will
stand it.'

'Oh !' said Foreman, gruffly ; 'they
know it won't last for long.   The people who

are rude to them this year, five years hence will be courting them.'

'You are quite right,' said Lord Aiden in a melancholy murmur. 'This rudeness is only the sacrifice which our fine people offer to their own self-respect. Think of the self-respect which such a sacrifice can propitiate!'

'At any rate,' said Carew, with a slight cynical laugh, 'they won't let their territory be invaded without a struggle.'

'The territory,' said Foreman, 'is only sticking out for the highest price it can get. But this,' he went on, 'is merely a side matter. The point is not that you truckle to their wealth—not even that you share it. The point is that you adopt their standards, which are the very inverse of your own, and that you are fast coming to measure all life by them. A man once had a stately dinner because he was a great man. Now he is a great man because he has a stately dinner.

That is the principle on which you countenance them ; and, having once accepted it, you have to apply it to yourselves. Here you have the reason why half the land of England is mortgaged. Think of this *bourgeoisie* which was once fawning at your feet ; and now you are ruining yourselves in order to feed it with truffles, or to avoid the shame of not eating so many truffles as it does.'

'Come,' said Mrs. Harley, 'I want you to tell me this. How does a man who draws an income, say from a brewery, differ from a man who has had just the same education, but happens to draw his income from an old landed property ? Would you really wish that from a mere sense of pride the one should refuse to associate on equal terms with the other ? '

'They don't differ,' said Foreman, 'except superficially. That is the very point I am arguing.'

'Well,' said Mrs. Harley, 'and how should they, or could they?'

'They can't,' said Foreman. 'That is, again, my point. Revolutions, as I told you, are not made by individuals; and the social change which we are now speaking of is only a fragment of a change that is far wider. No; our aristocracy and our *bourgeoisie* don't differ, except superficially; and it is absurd for the one to affect to despise the other, because it is absurd to believe that an aristocracy any longer really exists. There are but two classes in the world—labourers, and those who traffic in labour.'

'What, then, Mr. Foreman,' said Lady Chislehurst, a little severely, 'can you possibly mean by what you just now told us about Radicalism? You told us that the motive of the rich Radical classes was nothing but envy of this same non-existent aristocracy.'

'When I spoke,' replied Foreman, 'of our aristocracy as having ceased to exist, remember, please, that I added this saving clause. I said—I even urged—that it still retained its appearance, which, though not a sham, and when gone quite irreplaceable, is all the same a mere dying survival. Still, it is this—this shadow, this phantom—which our rich *bourgeoisie* envy; but envy is a passion which shows itself in two opposite ways. The retired huckster who spends five thousand pounds on hanging a ball-room with roses, in the hope that countesses will dance in it—his is an ambition which is petty and ignoble enough. But make his ambition still more intense and sensitive, make it ten times more abject, ten times more grovelling, and then it inverts itself, and turns into rancorous hatred. The orators who are so anxious to rob the lords of their coronets are the very men who, had the opportunity only come to them, would have given their eyes to boast about " My intimate friend Lord So-and-so." '

' That,' said Lord Aiden, ' I am sure, is perfectly true.'

' And I can give you, my lord,' said Foreman, ' one piece of comfort at least. Before Mr. Snapper relieves you of your lordship's coronet, we shall have relieved Mr. Snapper of many things far more substantial.'

' Now, Mr. Foreman,' said Mrs. Harley, ' although you are a Revolutionist, you must not forget you are an invalid ; and society itself, though it is only as old as civilization, is hardly more easy to upset than your health at the present moment. So you must let me remind you that it is already past your bedtime.'

' You're very kind to me,' said Foreman, with real gratitude in his voice.

' I'll tell you what I am,' said Mrs.

Harley. 'I'm very much provoked at you. It's all very fine to denounce the *bourgeoisie*, as you call them. But why should not Mr. Snapper, if he uses his wealth well, be as useful to England under Queen Victoria as ever was any baron before the Wars of the Roses? Mr. Stanley asked you that very question just now——'

'Yes,' said Foreman, looking about him eagerly, 'and would you really listen to me if I gave you the full answer? If so, you shall hear a few more truths to-morrow.'

'Do you know,' said Harley, as soon as Foreman was out of the room, 'there's a good bit of shrewdness in some of the things he says.'

'You mean,' said Lord Aiden, 'about Radicalism, and fine ladies, and ball-rooms?'

'All that,' said Mrs. Harley, 'about ball-rooms hung with roses—poor Foreman, I don't suppose he was ever in a ball-room in his life—it's all true in a way, but of course it's out of proportion.'

' The simple fact of the matter,' said Lord Aiden, ' is this. He makes the mistake of every theorist who approaches a life with which he is not familiar, and thinks he can understand it by the aid of his general principles. One can do that with no high society —least of all with English. The relation that prevails, and indeed has always prevailed in England, between birth and riches, between rank, power, and talent, may not, perhaps, be the most important problem in the world ; but, excepting Chinese grammar, I doubt if anything is more complicated ; and a judgment on it that even approaches truth is as nice a thing as the most delicate chemical compound. It is a mental secretion rather than a mental achievement. It is easy to learn principles ; the problem is how to apply them. They themselves may possibly never change ; but the circumstances they apply to are rarely in two cases the same ; and our social judgments, and much of what we mean by good-breeding, are a constant process of instinctive casuistry.'

' Precisely,' said Mr. Stanley. ' A man is no nearer being well-bred from having learnt the rules of an etiquette book, than he is nearer being a saint from knowing the ten commandments. And,' he added, smiling, ' as for our friend Mr. Foreman, what he says may be shrewd enough here and there ; but taking as a whole his views of the wealthier classes, his own manners, I expect, are more like those of a dandy than his judgment of the dandy's position could be like the actual truth.'

' Well,' said Carew, ' we shall see what he will tell us to-morrow.'

' And you too, Mr. Carew,' exclaimed Lady Chislehurst, ' you mustn't forget that you still owe us a debt. Do you remember your promise to tell us something about yourself, and some little mystery that employs you here at the château ? My dear,' she whispered to Miss Consuelo Burton, ' my own belief is, he's preparing himself for becoming a Catholic.'

' Foreman,' said Carew, ' leaves us tomorrow afternoon. When he is gone I shall be pleased to show you my mystery.'

CHAPTER X.

NEITHER Foreman nor Lady Mangotsfield had so absorbed the attention of everybody as to prevent the arrangements being made that came so near Lady Chislehurst's heart for the celebration next morning of early Mass in the chapel ; and the servants for the occasion deserting the village church, there was present a very respectable congregation. To Lady Chislehurst's extreme delight, Carew was amongst the number ; though could she have read the inner thoughts of his heart, she would have seen in what brought him there some cause for disappointment. He came less in the hopes of being touched by the sacred rite himself, than for the sake of observing the demeanour of Miss Consuelo Burton.

On a similar occasion, unknown to her, he had once before watched her at the Brompton Oratory; and the sight of her there had left behind it an image which, whenever he thought of it, gave a secret elevation to his life. And could it be, he had now lately asked himself, could it be that this vision, this faith was leaving her, which had once almost awed him, as though she were a superior being, and yet, at the same time, had somehow suggested help to him? Much of what she had said during the last few days seemed to hint this; and as, from a shadowy corner, he now fixed his eyes on her, he watched with a feeling of apprehensive sadness to detect some signs in her of a difference from her former self. And such signs, without doubt, he did detect; but they were not of the kind he had anticipated. What was his surprise when, instead of seeing, as he was prepared to see, that the devotion once so fervent had become lukewarm and perfunctory, he grew gradually to realize more and more that, if signs meant anything, it had grown and not lost in intensity! This was the girl who, only the day before, had seemed to be complaining that the chief of her Church's sacraments had ceased for her to have any saving virtue. Carew, as he watched her, felt more strongly than ever as if, through her, he were somehow placed in the presence of a power, a life, and a help which, to his own eye, was hidden; and when she rose finally, and was about to leave the chapel, her dark eyes, as she raised them towards the dingy window, seemed to have another light in them beyond what came through the cobwebs, and there was a glimmer in them as of tears that had just been shed secretly.

'Well,' said Lady Chislehurst as she met him in the passage afterwards, 'I am glad, Mr. Carew, to have seen you here this morning.'

'Next,' said Carew, ' to saying a prayer oneself, the best thing is to watch a good Catholic praying.'

Lady Chislehurst answered this with a glance of benediction and encouragement ; and then for an instant laying her hand on his arm, ' Did you see,' she said, ' someone else, who was present in the gallery ? I could hardly believe my eyes : it was actually Mr. Foreman.'

At this very moment Foreman himself appeared, having emerged from a narrow staircase.

' Mr. Foreman!' exclaimed Lady Chislehurst, 'allow me to congratulate you on the way in which you have begun your Sunday.'

'Oh,' said Foreman, with a bland and

careless laugh, ' I watch beliefs just as I watch classes. Besides, to-day I was doing what is merely an act of justice. I have been listening to you because you have promised to listen to me.'

At breakfast, Lady Mangotsfield being safe with an egg in bed, Mr. Stanley recurred to this same subject. 'Mr. Foreman,' he said, ' must remember what lies before him. He promised to tell us why what he calls the *bourgeoisie* can never succeed to the part that was once played by the aristocracy. I have a special curiosity to hear what he says on this point ; so I, for one, shall be no party to excusing him.'

Foreman was flattered to find he had roused such interest ; but he experienced a sensation of somewhat uneasy surprise at the critical tone which his ear seemed to catch in Mr. Stanley's manner of speaking about his ' special curiosity.' ' What,' thought Foreman, 'can this man, who only an hour ago was muttering hocus pocus, in the dress of a mediæval conjurer—what can he know of the rights and the claims of Labour? What can he know of that coming social earthquake which will send his churches toppling like a house of cards?'

' I trust,' he said civilly, but with a slight accent of sarcasm, 'that you will not think, if I really try to explain myself, that I am engaging you on subjects not befitting the day.'

'On the contrary,' said Mr. Stanley, with the same note in his voice, which seemed to indicate that he was treading on familiar ground, 'if your theory, or if your religion—I suppose, Mr. Foreman, I may venture to call it a religion——'

' Certainly,' said Foreman ; 'and of a kind that will make martyrs.'

' Well,' said Mr. Stanley, ' if your religion

were true, I should regard it at once as an integral part of mine.'

' Do you think, sir,' said Foreman, ' that the two would agree together?'

' They would,' said Mr. Stanley, ' if the world were perfect ; and when the world is perfect they will.'

' Perhaps,' returned Foreman, ' you are hardly quite aware of what the principles of us Socialists are.'

' And for that reason,' said Mr. Stanley, ' we are so anxious that you should tell us.'

After breakfast Foreman's first proceeding was to beg Mrs. Harley to have a word in private with him.

' I have with me,' he said in a low confidential tone, ' a copy of the new Address which the League is printing by thousands, and distributing in all the poorer quarters in London. It has also been translated into French, and our executive committee has sent two thousand copies to Decazeville, and ten thousand to the men on strike in Belgium. It goes straight, and without any humbug, to the bottom of the matter; and as these people seem anxious to hear something more from me, I could give them a glimpse of the ground they are really standing on. Do you think they would listen to me? I don't want to convert them; it's of no possible moment whether they are converted or not, and I should be sorry to bore them when no good could come of it.'

'No, no,' said Mrs. Harley; 'let us have your address by all means. I will put it to them now, and I'm sure they will say the same. Mr. Carew, Lady Chislehurst, everybody: Mr. Foreman says, if you wish to hear more about Socialism he will read you a paper he has just written himself, and which will tell us all just what we want to hear from him.'

Everyone assented to this proposal with pleasure, and a servant was sent to Foreman's bedroom for a bag, which seemed when it appeared to be bulging with revolutionary literature.

'Holloa!' exclaimed Harley, 'hooray for the dynamite! Evelyn, why in the world have I been given this red pocket handkerchief? I'll give it to Foreman, and he shall use it as a flag.'

'Ah,' said Foreman with a grunt, 'you may laugh if you like now. But even now you'd perhaps not laugh so much could you only see a letter which I got this morning from Chicago.' And he pulled out and tapped an exceedingly dirty-looking envelope.

Meanwhile, however, he had been grubbing about in his bag, and at last he extracted from it, with a quiet triumphant smile, a limp printed document like an electioneering leaflet. By this time his congregation had gathered round him, the members varying in the depth and quality of their interest, but all possessed with the not unpleasant feeling that they were going to be given a peep into the mind of a real conspirator.

'What I am going to read,' began Fore-man, 'as I have just told Mrs. Harley, is de-signed for the poorest workmen.' But here he stopped ; his eyes seemed to be straying from the paper he was reading to another that was lying upon his knee. ' Perhaps,' he said, as he took up this latter, 'you will let me first add a word or two to something I said last night.'

All his audience looked at him, and they were surprised both in his voice and his expression to detect a softness that had hitherto been present in neither. ' We were talking,' he went on, 'about Thackeray, and the social facts which he represented. I have here an extract from the best of his books, though the least instructive—"Esmond"; and just as in most places he exhibits the meanest of all social emotions, so here he spreads out for us, as a soft bed to repose upon, the falsest and yet the most plausible of all the moral emotions. " Love," he writes — and the writing is pretty enough—"Love, *omnia vincit*, is immeasurably above all ambitions, more precious than wealth, more noble than name. He knows not life who knows not that ; he hath not felt the highest faculty of the soul who hath not enjoyed it. In the name of my wife I write the completion of hope and the summit of happiness. To have such love is the one blessing in comparison of which all earthly joy is of no value ; and to think of her is to praise God ! " '

' Beautiful ! ' said Lady Chislehurst.

' Why, that,' said Mrs. Harley, ' is my favourite bit in Thackeray. What have you to say against that ? '

'Pooh!' said Foreman. 'There is the fault of all religions. They keep you fiddling away with your own private emotions, dusting your own souls, and filling yourselves with ecstasy if none of the little Dresden-china virtues in them are broken. What right have you to think *that* the summit of happiness, when your neighbours are turned into brutes by despair or hunger next door to you? Give me the man whose only notion of love is derived from a sixpenny kiss and a pair of painted cheeks ; and if such a man remembers the crying misery of the poor, he's a better man, I say, than any others who forget it, even if they forget it in praising God for their wives.'

Lady Chislehurst's face became frigid with disapproval, and she cast an anxious glance towards Miss Consuelo Burton. Mr. Stanley then, who was sitting near Foreman, said something in a low tone to him, in which

Miss Consuelo's name occurred ; but it was evident that then he must have added something conciliating, for Foreman, dropping the paper he had just been glancing at, again took up the original one, and proposed to resume his reading. As for Miss Consuelo herself, Carew looked at her, and her eyes were fixed on Foreman, as if her very soul were in the words he had just uttered.

He was now beginning again.

'What I am going to read,' he repeated, ' is designed for the poorest workmen. It is therefore put as simply as possible, and every point is ignored except those which are absolutely necessary. Mr. Stanley looks at me as if he would ask, Necessary for what? I mean, necessary for this—for showing the wage-slave what is the real relation between the results of his labour, the wages by which his labour is bought, and the profits of the employer who buys it—the profits, or what is just the same thing, the interest on the capital, the shares, the investments which that employer manipulates. Think of that,' exclaimed Foreman, his face growing gradually — darker. ' Let every owner of personalty think of that ! Let every owner of land, which is now merely the least objectionable form of personalty, think of that ! And it will thus be seen that this little leaflet, these few little pages I am now going to read to you, goes straight to the root of the existing social misery, and also,' he added, giving his voice a sarcastic calmness, ' of the existing social order. Well, I begin my Address thus :

'*Fellow-citizen, working-man — no matter what you work at, working with your hands for daily wages: Have you ever known what it is to want for anything,—for a better meal, for a more wholesome lodging, for a bit of pleasure and leisure for yourself, your wife, and children ? Are you ever discontented with the squalid court into which the window of your one room opens? Do you ever think that tough meat twice a week, and on most days a herring and a dry crust of bread, is not quite all that a hard day's work should earn, in this land of fabulous plenty? If so, consider this question. It concerns you very nearly.*

' By what means do you live, if that can be called life which is only not starvation? The single dog's hole that you live in, the wretched food you eat, the very rags you stuff into the broken window-panes—to get even these you must give or sell something. They are not given to you out of good nature. Now, what is it that you do give or sell? Have you a balance at your banker's? Have you an estate in the country? Beyond the clothes on your back and a few chairs and blankets, do you possess anything at all? And were all these sold, would they feed and lodge you for a week? Not they. Suppose that for a week you were thrown out of

employment, what would your case be at the end of it? Would you have anything? Could any creature in the whole wide world be so wholly destitute, so wholly helpless as you?

'Do you see your nakedness? You possess absolutely nothing—nothing, and yet one thing. That thing is your labour—the power of your muscles, guided by the intelligence of your brain. It is your labour that you give and sell from day to day for your subsistence. Cease to labour, and if it were not for the workhouse you would die.

'And now turn from your own case—from your own one room—to that magnificent palace yonder. Look at the owner coming out of it, with a gorgeous flower in his button-hole, and about to enter his carriage. Consider him; take a good look at him. That man sleeps on the softest down. Every hour of the day, if he wishes it, he eats some costly dainty. He has thirty servants, who each eat more at a sitting

than you do in two whole days. The cornice round one of that man's rooms has cost as much as will be the total of all your life's earnings. Here then is a second question for you: How does this man live? To get all these countless, these incredible luxuries, he too must give or sell something. Nobody gives them to him out of good nature. We will tell you what he gives or sells. It is the same thing—the very same thing that you do—it is LABOUR.

' " Labour ! " you exclaim; " he never did a stroke of work in his life. Do his puffy white hands, covered with rings, look like it ? " My friend, you are quite right—he never did a stroke, as you say. Catch him ! And yet what he gives in exchange for all these luxuries is Labour. It is all he has got to give—Labour. And it is Labour just such as yours—the power of muscle, guided by the intelligence of a brain. But he differs from you in this point, and in this point only: the Labour he gives is not his

own, but it is yours. Yes, yours, and that of hundreds of others of your fellow-labourers. And how does he get this Labour, this use of your muscles and your intelligence? There is only one way in which he can possibly get it, and in that way he does get it. He STEALS it. How could he get it otherwise? Are you his property? What right has he to your labour?

' Perhaps a new idea like this frightens you. Perhaps you will say that this man lives on the profits of his capital. Well, if you like, you may say that; it is only a question of words. But we would advise you to use words which explain their meaning a little more clearly. We will give you some that do; and as to what our words mean, you will be in no doubt whatever. Capital—this Capital we hear so much about— is simply the thief's name for Accumulated Labour; and profits, or interest, is simply the thief's name for Stolen Labour.

' *Listen, friend. No doubt you have studied politics, and have heard a good deal about Party cries. Well, how does that which we have just said strike you as the material for a cry? Perhaps you have heard things like it in the speeches of various Radicals. If you have, it is only for this reason—that these Radicals, who profess to be such friends of yours, never mean what they say, and, in this case, have not understood what they say. How can we know this? you ask. We know it for a very good reason. The leaders of these same Radicals are the greatest Labour Thieves in England themselves, and, therefore, they cannot really be proclaiming to you the truth, which, if you once understood it, would put a stop to the entire work of their lives. The particular slave-driver who, you are no doubt told, will be in a few years the Radical Prime Minister, and whose own endeavours will be then to protect your interests, steals from you at the rate of three thousand pounds a month, and is always looking about for means which will enable him to go on stealing with greater and still greater security.   He calls this looking for sound investments.*

' If, then, you think that a cry against the Labour Thieves will be a good cry for the labouring classes to rally to, we agree with you. But do not confound it with the cries the Radicals offer you.   Their cries, even if they sound like ours, have nothing in common with it but the sound.   Their cries are clap-trap.   Ours, which we offer you, is truth.   Yes, my friend, truth. We do not commend it to you merely because it suggests hope to you, but because it is based on a truth which can be as clearly proved, and is as scientifically true, as any of those discoveries which have resulted in railways or the electric telegraph.   The political economists will not like it.   We do not expect they will; but in the course of a few years we shall have taught them to swallow it.   At first it will startle them.   It will

*startle them still more later on, when they see
what is the result of your acting on it—when they
see how very different their own lives are then,
and how different yours are, too. We think
that that will startle them.*

*'This, then, is the great truth which we want
you, as a working-man, as a man who works
for an employer, to grasp. The profits of that
employer, which make him a rich man, are simply thievings from your Labour, and he thieves
from you in this way: He only pays you a
quarter of what your Labour is worth. Every
time he gives you five-and-twenty shillings you
virtually have given him five pounds. You give
him a five-pound note, and he professes to give
you change for it. What he does give you is a
sovereign and five shillings. He quietly pockets
the rest, saying nothing to you about it. There
you have his profits.*

*'Think of this, and see if it is not true. Do
not say it is true before you have examined it.*

We want you, before you get the idea fixed in your head, to thoroughly examine it, so as to be able to explain it and show your friends that it is no mere idle talk. When once you have seen it, it is the clearest thing in the world.'

'Now,' said Foreman, 'looking up from his paper, 'we are coming to the great theorem of Revolutionary Economics—a discovery hardly known to our *bourgeois* politicians, but one beside which, for its practical import to society, those of Newton, of Darwin, of Watt himself, are insignificant. We come to Karl Marx's theorem as to the nature of profits or interest, or—to put the matter plainly—of the entire subsistence of the leisured and the propertied classes. This is the real dynamite that will shatter our existing civilization—this single economic discovery. Recollect I am putting it here in the simplest way possible ; and the land question—quite a secondary one—for the moment I omit altogether.'

'*Come*,' he went on, beginning again to read, '*take any case which as a workman you know by your own experience—one such case is just as good as another—in which you or your fellows make some given thing for a wage-payer. One example will be as good as a thousand.*

'*Let us take, say, a number of boots, which you are making for the owner of a large boot-shop. On what does that shopkeeper live, as he does live, in affluence? For he is affluent, compared with you, at any rate.*

'*Part of the answer is easy, and anybody can at once give it. He lives on the difference between what he gives you for making the boots and what his customers give him for them.*

'*Yes, but wait a bit. All that difference is not theft, and he does not live on the whole of it. Let us be quite just, and not jump too quickly at conclusions. The shopkeeper—let us put this point first—does some work on the boots, just as you do, before they are sold finally. He introduces your boots to the customer; he makes them marketable. This work is necessary, and he must be paid for it; though, as the work is easier than yours, he should, perhaps, be paid less. Of the difference, then, between the price he gets for the boots and the sum he pays you for making them we must credit him, to be generous, with a wage equal to yours. Be careful, however, to see what that means. It is faster work to sell boots than to make them, and he sells, we may suppose, in one day what it takes you six days to make. Thus, if the shopkeeper is to be fully occupied, he must employ six workmen, each of whom supplies him with boots for one day in the week. Since, then, he is entitled to the same weekly wage as you and your fellows, he is entitled, for selling your six days' Labour, to exactly one-sixth of what he pays you for it. If he gives you, say, five shillings a day, he is* entitled to five shillings a day himself. Thus, he is entitled to five shillings for selling what he pays you thirty shillings for making. You see, therefore, that what he pays you thirty shillings for making cannot possibly be sold to the customer for less than thirty-five shillings.

' It could not be sold for less. We must say more than that: it could not be sold for so little. Consider, the shopkeeper has to pay for the leather, and he has also to pay for his shop. The leather costs, we will say, as much as your own wages, namely, thirty shillings for the week; the rent of the shop for the day on which he sells your work is seven shillings. Here, then, is a total of thirty-seven shillings, which the shopkeeper, if he is to sell boots at all, must get back from the customer.

' Now, then, here is a little sum for you, which will explain your employer's position, so far as it has to do with you. Thirty shillings you receive for the making of so many boots ; your *employer must receive five shillings for selling them; he must receive, also, thirty shillings for the material, which he has bought, and seven shillings for the day's use of the shop—making in all seventy-two shillings. That is the minimum for which the boots could be sold; and, were they sold for that, the shopkeeper would be earning exactly what you earn. He would be living as you live, in one squalid room, tasting meat only twice a week. But does he live like that? Not he, as you know well enough. You know where his snug villa is, with its greenhouse, and its garden in front of it; and you have seen the chops and steaks which he has every day in the back parlour of his shop.*

' Here at last we come to the practical question for you—for you, the man who has stitched the boots—you through whose sweat and weariness the leather has become boots at all. How is it your employer lives as he does live—live so much better than you? How does he get the money

which enables him to do so? Let us see. Let us take a peep at his account-books, and they, we rather fancy, will throw a little light on the subject.

'His account-books tell us that he gets his money in this way—from selling the boots not for seventy-two shillings, but for a hundred and sixty shillings. Remember this too—he is able to sell the boots for that sum because they are worth it. If they were not worth it he could not get it. The competition of other shoemakers would pretty soon force his price down. Taking the shopkeepers of this country as a body, the average price charged by them, and got by them for their goods from the public, represents the value of those goods. Of those goods our boots are only a specimen.

'How, then, do the boots come to have the value above stated? What item is there in the cost of producing and selling them that we have not yet considered? The rent of the shop is seven shillings, the leather costs thirty shillings—that is

thirty-seven shillings. You merely have to add the shopkeeper's own wage, five shillings, and your wage, thirty shillings, making in all, seventy-two shillings; and yet the total result is a hundred and sixty shillings. There are eighty-eight shillings unaccounted for. Perhaps he bought the leather too cheap, or got his shop too cheap. Do you think that? Do landlords let their shops below the market price? Do leather-sellers let their customers have for thirty shillings what is really worth a hundred and eighteen? You know better than to believe that. Depend upon it your employer has paid for the house and the leather every penny that either of them is worth. Think! Do you smell a rat now? Does it strike you that there may still be something for which he has not paid so honestly? There is only one thing left, and that thing is your Labour.

'*There you have it. There is the thing which the eighty-eight shillings comes from. Your*

Labour, with your employer's added to it—for let us give the Devil his due, and let us remember his Labour also—this Labour is in reality worth, not thirty or thirty-five shillings, but it is worth a hundred and twenty-three shillings. Of this one-sixth belongs to him. What is one-sixth of that? Twenty shillings and sixpence. Give him that, and have done with him; and then what remains for you? Five pounds two shillings and sixpence. That is your just share; not thirty shillings. Thus your employer, every time he pays your weekly wage, underpays you by the difference between these two sums. That is to say, he robs you of three pounds twelve shillings and sixpence. He robs you of it, he pockets it, and then calls it his profits.

'Turn this thought over in your mind. Think of it at leisure; think of it in the workshop. Think of it when you have not a penny in your pocket, when you are hungry, when your wife and little children are hungry. Think

of it, above all, when your wages are being paid you. Every time your employer gives you thirty shillings, remember that you have in reality given him something like a five-pound note ; and that he is pocketing, that he is robbing you of, some three pounds ten of your change.

' In speaking to you, we have supposed you were a shoemaker. It is no matter what you are or whom you work for. If you are a bricklayer, a journeyman tailor, a hand in a factory, it is all the same thing. You, and all your fellow wage-slaves, numbering in this country some twenty-seven millions, are all in the same case. The propertied classes—your employers—one and all rob you.

' This is a great subject. We cannot put the whole of it to you in one pamphlet, but this one thought—the thought that you are robbed, that the propertied classes live on robbing you, and that all the other wrongs which politicians say they will remedy are nothing if this wrong is not

remedied—keep that in your own mind, and try to put it into the mind of your fellow wage-slaves; and remember, if you want any more information, you can have it at the office of the League of Social Democrats.

' If you would further your own cause, you are invited to join that League. The subscription is half a crown.'

'There!' exclaimed Foreman, dropping his paper, and looking round him. 'Does that satisfy you? Does that sound clear enough for you? I should like to know. Does it, or does it not?'

'Do you really mean to say,' exclaimed Lady Chislehurst, 'that you are trying to disseminate ideas like these amongst the working-classes—to fill them with such horrible feelings of envy, hatred, and discontent?'

'I do,' said Foreman, bringing his hand down on the arm of his chair with a thump; 'discontent with the lives they lead now, and hatred of those who force such a life upon them.'

'Then,' said Lady Chislehurst, 'I must tell you I consider it very wicked of you. You like plain speaking, Mr. Foreman, so you must not object to it in me.'

'Lady Chislehurst,' said Mrs. Harley in a whisper, ' don't make him angry, for pity's sake, or we shall have a scene in a moment. Haven't you watched his eyes? They have the regular tint of madness in them, and can't you see the excitement into which he's read himself? Listen—listen now. Your friend Mr. Stanley is at him.'

Mr. Stanley was speaking with a gentle, an almost timid courtesy. 'There was one point,' he said, ' in your paper, Mr. Foreman, on which I should like to question you. The wages paid to the supposed shoemaker, and the price of the leather used by him—were these real, or merely imaginary?'

'The figures quoted,' said Foreman, 'were as a fact imaginary ones. What the real figures would be I neither know nor care. These were chosen because they were easy to work with. Their actual accuracy,' he added brusquely, 'matters nothing at all to the argument.'

'Certainly not,' said Mr. Stanley, 'nothing at all. And now may I ask you this? Given the wages which you imagine the workmen to receive, was the proportion between those wages and the profits of the employer—between the thirty shillings and the three pounds twelve and sixpence—was that imaginary also? Or do you suppose it to represent a fact?'

Foreman stared at Mr. Stanley, not with anger exactly, but with excitement. 'I don't,' he said, 'suppose anything at all in the matter. That does represent a fact. There is no reason for supposing there.'

'But how,' said Mr. Stanley, 'since you are not aware of the exact wages that prevail in the shoe-trade, are you able to arrive at such exactness in this most important point?'

'In this way,' said Foreman, fumbling for something in his bag. 'In this way,' he went on, producing another leaflet. 'I will only read you a line or two. That will answer your question—

'*Workmen of England : Consider the following figures. The annual income of this country is thirteen hundred millions. All those thirteen hundred millions are made by your labour. Who gets them? What becomes of them? This becomes of them. Ten hundred millions are appropriated, are nabbed, by your employers, the drones, the propertied classes. Three hundred millions only are left for you— for you—you, who have. made the whole of it. Think of these figures. Think of them! Think of them!! Think of them!!!*'

'There,' said Foreman, ' is the basis of my calculation as to the shoe-trade. These figures show you the broad facts of the case. Take the workers of this country as a whole, and their employers—the drone-classes—as a whole ; and the latter fleece the former to the tune of ten pounds out of every thirteen. In my case of the shoe-trade, if I err at all, I err in putting the shopkeeper's legitimate gains too high.'

' May I,' said Miss Consuelo Burton, 'look at that last leaflet, Mr. Foreman ? '

Surprise and gratification came into Foreman's eyes. He handed her the leaflet, and was about to begin addressing her, when an ill-timed remark from Lord Aiden completely diverted him from his intention.

' It seems,' said Lord Aiden, in an accent of lazy thoughtfulness, ' that you take no account of the interest yielded by capital.'

For a few moments Foreman was absolutely silent. He stared at Lord Aiden much in the same way as he had stared at Mr. Stanley; only this time his excitement was greater, and there seemed something in it almost ferocious. At last the storm broke.

'Interest!' he exclaimed, hissing with nervous vehemence. 'Capital bear interest! That is the very lie I am unmasking. It is the thief's lie—the swindler's lie. It is the lie on which the propertied classes repose, and under which the working-classes are crushed. Interest, the swindlers tell you, is a plant that grows out of capital. Fools! It no more grows out of capital than corn grows from a spade. It grows out of labour, as all wealth grows; and it is merely the name for the part of the growth you steal. Of course,' Foreman went on, his tone growing contemptuous rather than angry, 'to understand the matter scientifically, one must understand the nature of Values. But first let the workman digest the notion that he is plundered, and then if he is inclined to doubt it, we will take care to prove to him that his notion is correct.'

' My dear Lady Chislehurst,' Mrs. Harley was saying meanwhile, ' I believe all this no more than you do. Can't you see that the poor creature's a madman ? Dangerous ? Yes ; no doubt this teaching is dangerous ; but it's just as well to realize what it is.'

' I am sorry,' said Lady Chislehurst, 'that Consuelo thinks so, at any rate. That man seems quite to have bewitched her.'

Mrs. Harley looked to see if this observation was justified ; and the *tableau* that met her view made her think that perhaps it was. Miss Consuelo Burton had risen from her seat, and, looking very pretty in the neatest of neat dresses, was standing by Foreman's chair, with one slim hand on the back of it, and her eyes and voice at once were making some request of him. ' Mr. Foreman,' she was saying, 'may I see that other paper of yours also—the one you first read out to us ? There are one or two things in it which I did not quite follow, I think.'

Foreman did not need to be asked twice. The look of ferocity died away from his face, and a gleam succeeded it of odd innocent vanity. He seemed quite subdued by the graceful form that bent over him, and the voice that, with all its timidity, had a subtle note of command in it. 'Keep the papers,' he said; 'you can have as many copies as you like. Here, too, is another, about "Value and Capital." You had better take that as well.'

She took the two papers, and retiring into a distant window, to Lady Chislehurst's horror, was at once completely absorbed in them.

'I think, Mr. Foreman,' said Mr. Stanley, 'that if I wished to teach your lesson to the working-classes, I should have administered the paper on Value as the first dose, not the second.'

'You do!' exclaimed Foreman, with a start of suspicious astonishment, which seemed partly caused by the priest's having any opinion on the matter, partly by his decided and calm way of expressing it. 'And may I venture to ask, sir, why?'

'But, Mr. Stanley,' said Lord Aiden, 'you would surely not personally be for teaching these theories to the working-classes at all?'

'I think,' said Mr. Stanley, 'that if you take these theories as a whole, in sober earnest, there are only two defects in them.'

'My dear sir,' said Foreman, 'you are very good, I am sure. But permit me to remark, you have not yet heard the whole of them— not even in outline; and even if you had, you could hardly pronounce on them, or even fully understand them, off-hand.'

'In that,' said Mr. Stanley, 'I am sure you are perfectly right, and I fear I must seem to you presumptuous, or perhaps even impertinent. But I assure you, Mr. Foreman, that I should not have ventured on my criticism if the subject had not been one with which—if I may have your permission to say so—I am as familiar as you yourself are.'

Foreman sat up in his chair, bending his head forward. 'Excuse me,' he said, almost stuttering in his eagerness, 'excuse me, Mr. Stanley, but no one can be familiar with this subject we are speaking about who has studied social problems under Catholic—under clerical authorities. No one who has not mastered a work almost unknown in England—the epoch-making work of Karl Marx on " Capital "—no one, I say——' he repeated, pausing with an air of triumph.

'Again,' said Mr. Stanley, 'I agree with you perfectly ; for there is no work in the

English language with which I am so familiar as that special work you refer to.'

'The work I refer to,' retorted Foreman, 'happens to be in German, and no English translation has ever yet been published. I much fear we are talking at cross purposes.'

'I think not,' replied Mr. Stanley, smiling. 'What I said just now was perhaps a slip of the tongue ; and yet it was more accurate than you could know it to be. No English translation of Marx has been published—that is quite true. One has been made, however, and will be published shortly, with notes on the author's fallacies.'

'Indeed!' said Foreman. 'And may I ask you by what translator ? '

'Myself,' said Mr. Stanley dryly.

Over Foreman's face there came a dull cloud of mortification. He leant back again, and said with a forced air of indifference,

' Perhaps, then, you will kindly tell me what are the two defects in the system of Karl Marx, which you spoke of.'

' I charge Marx,' said Mr. Stanley, ' with only one of them. I will talk about that presently. The other—forgive me for saying so —is an error which must be mainly your own. The figures you quote with regard to the distribution of wealth in this kingdom, and which you rely on to arouse in the workman a sense of social injustice—they refer, I conclude, to the present time, do they not ? '

' They do,' said Foreman, ' and you are right—the figures are mine.'

' Well,' said Mr. Stanley, with almost apologetic civility, ' if you will go into the matter a little more carefully, with a little method, and access to the best authorities, you will find that your present calculations are— and we should be thankful for it—so far in error, that they do not represent even an approximation to the truth.'

The cloud upon Foreman's face grew duller and more lowering. 'Are you at all aware,' he exclaimed, speaking with difficulty, 'are you at all aware who I am ?—who it is who is sitting in this chair here ? Perhaps you do not know that for the past ten years I have done nothing but study the misery of the working-classes—aye, Mr. Stanley, and in the very scenes and times of their misery ; and not there only. I have ransacked your Blue-books and your Parliamentary returns, and with the aid of the first statistician in England I have ranged my facts and ranged my figures in order. There is only one other man in existence who knows as much of the subject as I do, and that is the man from whom my figures are taken. He, Mr. Stanley, is Mr. Charles Griffen, the statistical secretary to the Inland Revenue

Office. Do you admit Mr. Griffen to be an authority ? Or, possibly, you have never heard of him.'

' No, no,' said Mr. Stanley ; ' Mr. Griffen is a most undoubted authority ! '

' Well,' said Foreman, ' as I tell you, it is from him my figures are taken. They are taken from his various Abstracts and Essays, and are put together by myself. Mr. Griffen, you may not be aware, has from his official position sources of information almost unique in their completeness, and accessible to him alone. The results he is deducing from these are not yet made public. When they are, of course, they will be more detailed than mine ; but nothing can make them differ from mine substantially, though what his details will be we shall none of us know till he publishes them.'

' Do you know Mr. Griffen personally ? ' said Mr. Stanley.

'No,' replied Foreman.

'It happens,' said Mr. Stanley, 'that I do. I have been over the proofs of this very work of his you are alluding to; in fact, he was good enough to entrust me with the correction of them.'

'Figures,' exclaimed Foreman savagely, 'can be made to prove anything, that is to say on paper. Let me see Mr. Griffen's figures, and I will engage to make good my own case from them—let the figures be what they may. You come with me into the workman's quarters, and then doubt me if you can. Have I worked for ten years amongst the wage-slaves of England, and yet cannot be sure of the simple fact which I tell you—that out of every thirteen pounds the wage-slaves produce, the capitalistic classes rob them of ten pounds? That is, I repeat, the proportion, and no juggling with arithmetic can alter it.'

'Well,' said Mr. Stanley, 'since we cannot agree about England, let us turn to some other country. Do you consider that the same thing holds good everywhere? Does it hold good, for instance, in America? I am told that if the workmen in England get little, in America they get still less.'

'Less than ours in England?' said Foreman. 'If they did they would starve. In England the workmen live on starvation wages. Who will venture to tell you that anywhere they can live on less than that?'

'Let us reduce the affair to dollars,' said Mr. Stanley. 'In a dollar there are a hundred cents. Out of every dollar the English workman makes, the capitalist, according to you, takes about seventy-seven cents, and leaves him about twenty-three. Such is your computation. Well, in America, I am told that out of every dollar the workman produces, the capitalist takes ninety-four and leaves him six.'

'What fool,' exclaimed Foreman, 'can have possibly told such stuff to you? And do you mean to say you believed it?'

'No,' said Mr. Stanley. 'I have not admitted that. But the person who made the statement holds a position, and claims a species of knowledge not unlike your own. You spoke, Mr. Foreman, just now of Chicago. The person I quote from is a certain Heinrich Jungbluth, the leader and organizer of the Chicago band of Socialists. He has stated in a leaflet not unlike one of your own that the American workman, for every dollar he makes, gets himself exactly six cents.'

The fashion of Foreman's countenance underwent a sudden change. His jaw fell. He appeared to be almost terrified.

'Heinrich Jungbluth!' he exclaimed. 'And what do you know about Heinrich Jungbluth?'

'Several things,' said Mr. Stanley, 'if you care to hear them. He was a clerk originally in a commercial house in Paris, but was dismissed in consequence of some disgraceful scandal. Subsequently he came to America, and took a prominent part in the Pittsburg riots. At one time he was suspected of having forged a cheque. At another time he was sent to prison for a violent assault upon a woman. He is now the corresponding member of the League of Social Democrats, and is urging them at this moment to attempt some outbreak in London.'

'Who are you?' shouted Foreman. 'Are you a Socialist yourself in disguise? Let me look at you. Have I ever seen you before?'

'No,' said Mr. Stanley. 'I am a priest of the Catholic Church—a league, if you like to call it so, even more far-reaching than yours ; and we too have our correspondents in all parts of the world. Let us say no more, however, about Herr Jungbluth's character. I merely mentioned his statistics, which you say are impossible, to show you that Socialism does not always insure accuracy.'

' God bless my soul, sir!' said Foreman, ' if you understand the matter so much better than I do, I can only say you had better become a Socialist, since you tell me you are not one already.'

' Let us forget,' said Mr. Stanley, ' the point on which we differ personally. In spite of that even I would willingly be a Socialist, if it were not for the other fatal defect I spoke of—the defect in the theory, as apart from the statistics of Socialism.'

' Well,' said Foreman, sulkily, ' you seem so singularly conversant with the entire question that I cannot but be curious—very curious indeed—to learn from you what this fatal defect may be.'

' Put briefly,' said Mr. Stanley, who was now the centre of attention, ' it is this : not that your theory is in any place inconsistent with itself, but that it is quite inapplicable to ordinary human nature. Were we all of us angels, your economic system would be perfect ; and if we lapsed afterwards into capitalists you might properly call us devils. As it is, we are men, with men's powers and motives, which must be indeed controlled, but can never be fundamentally altered. If your economic system does not apply to these it applies to nothing, and has no practical meaning. What I say is, that your system does not apply to them. Allow me to ask you this : you are not a believer, I think, in what are called natural rights, are you ? '

' Certainly not,' said Foreman. ' Natural

rights imply some supernatural sanction; and whatever Socialists individually may think as to religious matters, their economic system has nothing to do with religion. Our basis is social rights, not any such nonsense as natural rights.'

'Precisely,' said Mr. Stanley. 'Your position, I think, is this. Men have no right to anything which they have no means of keeping; and no right to anything which there is no possibility of their getting. Thus they have no right to any property in the wind, and they have no right to any property in the moon.'

'Of course,' said Foreman, impatiently, 'we all of us know that.'

'Well, Mr. Foreman, let us now go to practical matters. Let me ask you if you agree to this: capital is essential to production—we may call it, in fact, the means of production; and, were capital destroyed altogether, the working-classes would suffer even more than they do from its being kept as it is, in the hands of a few capitalists.'

'Naturally,' said Foreman; 'that is the key to the whole position. Capital is not merely the means of production. It is the means of life; and it is because the means of life have been monopolized by that small ring which we call the capitalists that these capitalists are able to dictate terms to the workers.'

'That is to say,' said Mr. Stanley, 'the workers must either starve, or work for the capitalists; and the capitalists pay them, not what their work is worth, but only just enough of its worth to keep them in working order, and to make life seem a better thing than death to them. The remainder is appropriated—as you would say, stolen—by the capitalists; and they are only able to steal it because they have monopolized the capital.

Now, Mr. Foreman, if you put the case like that, up to this point I altogether agree with you.'

'You do!' exclaimed Foreman. 'Well, sir, and what next?'

'I agree with you, further,' Mr. Stanley continued, 'in this. Could it be brought about that there were no such monopoly, and if the community possessed the capital in common, the workers would themselves receive the whole of what they have had a hand in producing. The capitalists, to borrow your language, would not be able to steal any profits from them. Here, then, we come, I think, to the sum of the Socialistic gospel. *The workers have a right to the capital of the community.*'

'Certainly,' said Foreman. 'That is substantially what we say.'

'Now here, at last,' replied Mr. Stanley, 'is the point where we part company. I say just the reverse. I say the capitalists have a right to what you call their thievings. I don't expect to convince you ; but I can, if you will listen to me, explain to you what I mean, and at all events you will find in it something to think of. We agree—don't we ?—upon two points as to capital. It is necessary to the workers; there is one point. It is accumulated labour; there is the other point. Well, I say that the capitalists have a right to their thievings, because if it were not for the sake of these thievings the capital would never have been accumulated ; and that the workers at large have no right to the capital, because, if they seized on it they would be unable to keep it. It has only — Mr. Foreman, pray let me finish what I am saying—capital has only been accumulated under the direction of a minority. It would begin to disappear the very moment it ceased to be properly admin-istered ; and no one is able to administer it properly except those who are certain to profit by its administration. There, Mr. Foreman, you have my meaning in outline. If we were all equally clever and all equally industrious, your theory would be perfect. The State would be Socialistic to-morrow. There is only one other supposition on which the same result would be possible.'

'And what is that?' said the voice of Miss Consuelo Burton, who had again joined the group, and for some time past had been listening.

'It would be possible,' said Mr. Stanley, 'if the average race of men were all of them to rise to heights of zeal and self-sacrifice to which saints and heroes at present find it very hard to attain. Will Mr. Foreman allow me to ask him one question more? The kind of life you contemplate in your Socialistic state is one of enjoyment, comfort, cheerfulness, and so forth, is it not? It does not, at all events, approach the gloom and the hard discipline of the severe monastic orders ? Exactly. I thought so. I have known other men, of views similar to yours, and they have all declared that the asceticism of the Christian Church is little less than a blasphemy against our healthy human nature.'

'How can Mr. Stanley allude to such opinions in such company?' Lady Chislehurst said to herself in a troubled half-audible murmur.

'Fasting, for instance, and celibacy,' Mr. Stanley was meanwhile proceeding, 'the violent mortification, and, above all. the suppression of any natural appetite, men of Mr. Foreman's school think terrible—tending, in fact, to produce every form of evil.'

'There,' said Foreman dryly, 'you do me complete justice.'

'You are doubtless aware, Mr. Foreman, that this discipline in its severest form is regarded by the Catholic Church as fitted only for a very small fraction of mankind. What I want to say to you is, that the severest discipline ever devised for any handful of monks does far less violence to our average human nature than the change in it which your system would require to be universal. It would be easier, far easier, to make men Trappists than Socialists.'

Foreman had come to the château expecting some discussion, and he was fully prepared to startle and horrify everybody. Some cross-questionings, some panic-stricken contradictions, he anticipated ; and he pictured himself like a war-horse riding them down and dispersing them. But that he should meet with anyone to whom his arguments were familiar beforehand, and who, instead of being frightened and shocked at them, was able to dispute them in detail, and make him exchange his thundering rhetorical charge for a slow argumentative walk, in which he was answered at every step—for such a contingency he was utterly unprepared; and he now sat feeling almost as dizzy as if his chair had suddenly broken and he had fallen bang on the floor.

In this state of mind, though he hated footmen on principle, he had never been so near to thinking he had seen an angel as he was now, at the entrance of Lady Mangotsfield's superb attendant, who threw the whole question of the rights of the masses into the background, by the announcement that her ladyship was at breakfast in the east *salon*, and before her departure, in half an hour's time, would be very much pleased to say good-bye to her friends. 'I was to say,' the man added, 'that her ladyship particularly hopes that Mr. Foreman will see her ladyship.'

At this last announcement a smile went the round of the company, in which Foreman himself joined, though with anything but good humour. He had by this time recovered his self-possession ; and though he had not by any means collected and got into fighting order his arguments, which had been scattered by Mr. Stanley's attack to the farthest confines of his mind, he found himself fortified by a fit of gathering anger, and this showed itself at the very first opportunity. The party were now preparing to break up ; but the subject just discussed still held their attention ; and Lord Aiden, turning to Foreman, said in a conciliatory way :

'Of course the practical point for us who do not agree with you, is not so much whether your opinions are true as whether they are in reality spreading much amongst the people.'

'You are right there, my lord,' said Foreman ; 'and the rate at which these opinions spread amongst the people varies with the acuteness of industrial distress or depression. I'm not a man who is squeamish

about a simile, and I don't mind saying that
Socialism is for all the world like yellow fever
or the cholera. It is propagated by germs;
only in this case the germs are knowledge,
often disseminated in the form of mere leaflets.
What I have just read you is one of them. I
think, Mr. Stanley, you will by-and-by have
a practical lesson as to whether Socialism is
really inapplicable to ordinary human nature
or not. Listen : can you deny this? Take
any audience of working-men you like—let
them call themselves Radicals, let them call
themselves Conservatives ; what they are
really brooding over is a sense of the same
social injustice. They feel it, but they can't
define it. Socialism defines it for them.
When they realize the definition then the
disease is taken.'

'Your similes,' said Harley, 'don't flatter
your arguments.'

'They don't,' said Foreman. 'They are

not meant to do so. You don't flatter the Devil if you want to describe him, do you? And from your point of view—I am quite aware of this—my opinions are far uglier than any devil you believe in. Yes,' exclaimed Foreman, 'and they'll be playing the devil soon, inapplicable as they are to average human nature, with most of the things that propertied human nature lives by.'

'My dear Foreman,' exclaimed Harley, with a genial burst of laughter, 'upon my word you are quite delightful.'

Foreman was in no mood to be joked with by even his oldest friends. He sat up in his chair like an adder about to spring.

'Come,' said Lady Chislehurst, carefully looking away from him, ' Mr. Carew is gone to Lady Mangotsfield; let us all of us go too.'

'Listen!' exclaimed Foreman, in a voice that suddenly arrested them ; ' before you go, let me tell you all this: and before a fortnight's over you will see whether I am a liar or no. By that time Socialism will either speak with fifteen mouths at St. Stephen's, or it will be speaking with a great many more, and with louder mouths, in the streets!'

At this moment the door of the room opened, and a tremulous but distinct voice was heard outside in the passage. 'Mr. Carew,' it was saying, ' and where is that odd creature—poor Lord B——'s Conservative? He goes back to Nice himself, don't he, to-day? Tell him to come in my carriage, and I'll give a little advice to him.'

Lady Chislehurst rustled towards the door with the instinctive intention of arresting Lady Mangotsfield's remarks about a person who could hear every word of them. It may safely be said, however, that she did not break her heart when, before she could accomplish her purpose, Lady Mangotsfield went on again, and said in a voice that must have been still more distinct to Foreman, 'Of course if people of that sort must meddle in politics it's all the better that they should be on the right side ; but I often think of what I once said to my gardener, who was always teasing me with the ardour of his Tory principles. "Macdonald," I said, " I'm very glad you hold sound opinions ; but I'd far rather that you had no opinions at all." '

CHAPTER XI.

ADY MANGOTSFIELD was gone. Foreman was going. With Lady Mangotsfield he was not in the least angry. He was even pleased with the view which she took of his own position—a view which to him was as picturesque as a ruined castle, and as harmless. He had no inclination, however, for the high honour of travelling with her ; and as soon as ever her postchaise had departed, his own humble vehicle drew up at the archway. It was close upon one o'clock. He was begged to stay to luncheon ; but the prophetic rage, which was not quite devoid of sullenness, was upon him ; and, putting a constraint on his appetite, although it happened to be voracious, he declined all refreshments except a few solitary biscuits ; and even the dust of these, as he went, shook off as a testimony.

'Well,' said Mrs. Harley, who walked out with him to the carriage, 'I think, Mr. Foreman, you have met your match to-day.'

'I suppose,' he said, 'you are alluding to that priest. I was certainly surprised to find that he knows as much of the question as he does ; though I could show him, if I had the time, that he knows rather less than he thinks. As for the others—I don't suppose there is one of them who has thought enough to have any real opinion about it at all.'

'And so,' said Carew at luncheon, 'the prophet has come and gone ! '

There was an inexpressible relief amongst all present at the thought ; and Carew and

Mrs. Harley began to congratulate each other that things had not gone off as badly as they easily might have done.

' Don't you think,' interposed Lady Chislehurst, ' that he's a very horrible man? If he's as bad as he makes himself out to be, he is little better than a criminal. He's trying to bring about those very horrors which he pretends to think are inevitable.'

' He's a product,' said Mr. Stanley, ' of many social conditions, and represents—depend upon it—certain very important forces. I have long watched the ways of the Socialists carefully, but had not come across Mr. Foreman's track before.'

' My dear Mr. Stanley,' said Lady Chislehurst, ' you don't really think that these men can do anything ? '

' I,' said Carew, ' am not at all so certain of that. In London alone they have every material for a rising ; and they may make a

massacre, though they will never make a mil-
lenium. Mrs. Harley, what wine are you
drinking ?'

'I must confess,' said Lady Chislehurst,
'you take things very coolly, Mr. Carew.'

'After all,' he said, 'what does it matter ?
Life as it is—apart from religion, I mean—is a
bad thing at the best ; and human beings are
contemptible little animals.'

'And yet,' said Miss Consuelo Burton,
'you think so much of our aristocracy—you
think them, Mr. Carew, such a very superior
order of beings.'

'Everything,' said Carew, 'is comparative.
They are clean when compared to dirt. An
aristocracy—this at least is what I feel—is
the best of all possible orders in the worst of
all possible worlds.'

'And so,' said Mrs. Harley, 'the people
are dirt, are they ? I thought, Mr. Carew, you
were so devoted to improving their condition.'

'They are only dirt,' said Carew, 'when they seize on power. We are dirt when we relinquish it. Soup is dirt on your pocket-handkerchief; your pocket-handkerchief is dirt in the soup-tureen.'

'Well,' said Mrs. Harley, 'if those are your political opinions, there won't be very much power, in these popular days, for you.'

'They are not my opinions,' said Carew; 'they are my feelings—which is a very different thing. My political opinions are my political feelings criticised.'

During the rest of luncheon, Miss Consuelo Burton was silent. Whether Foreman was right or no with regard to most of the others, when he said that as to his views they had no real opinion, with regard to Miss Consuelo he was certainly quite wrong. She had an opinion that was very real indeed, and with that tact which rarely deserts a woman until she is so much in love that her happiness hangs upon its exercise, she contrived, during the course of a walk in the afternoon, to secure Mr. Stanley for a time as her sole companion, on purpose to communicate this opinion to him.

In all the landscape commanded by the ramparts of the château, the most singular object, perhaps, was a certain solitary tower which rose out of the foliage of a semi-precipitous forest, and seemed to be guarding the entrance to a winding valley. It was the one remnant of a stronghold that had formerly belonged to the Templars ; and it had been partly repaired by the Comte de Courbon-Loubet, and converted by him into a memorial to his lost children. Its distance from the château was not more than two miles, and as soon as the party had recovered from the lulling effects of luncheon, it was to this tower they all set out on foot.

Mr. Stanley and his companion were the

first to arrive at it ; and whilst the others were still far below them, waging a dilatory battle with the thick and refractory underwood, they themselves were already quietly seated at the top of a flight of steps by which the base of the tower was reached. They exchanged a few remarks about the building and the scene around them. Then Miss Consuelo abruptly changed the subject, and said, somewhat to Mr. Stanley's surprise :

' I saw the other day an odd thing in a newspaper. I saw that of all the kinds of books published in England annually, those on religion were by far the most numerous. The reason is, I suppose, that although the subject is dry, yet, to those who care at all for it, it is the most important subject in life.'

' One is,' said Mr. Stanley, ' sometimes apt to forget what an enormous body the reading public is, and that only a small section of it reads mainly for amusement. The bulk of the middle and lower middle classes, when they do read, read with the serious aim of instructing themselves.'

'I'm not surprised,' said Miss Consuelo, 'that so dry a subject should be popular; but that the general public don't take to a dryer one. If I were the general public, I know I would. I would think about nothing else—nothing, nothing, nothing! I would,' she exclaimed, as if carried away by her feelings, 'I would shut up all my books on religion; and—and this other subject—till I knew and felt at rest about it, I could never open any one of them again.'

Her cheeks were flushed, and her eyes were fixed on the priest. She seemed to be half afraid of the words she had just spoken. 'Tell me,' he said, 'and what subject is this, which is so much more important to your own life than religion is?'

She paused for a moment as if not quite

sure of her voice. At last she spoke, and there came into her eyes as she did so a spark of vanishing laughter. 'Of course,' she began, 'when I tell it to you, it sounds not only wicked but ridiculous. The subject I mean is — don't laugh at me — it is Political Economy.'

Mr. Stanley looked at her, with a smile that was certainly not one of ridicule.

'What was the man's name,' she went on, 'that you and Mr. Foreman talked about? Karl Marx—yes, that's it. Why don't people in general study books like his, and see if they're true or not, or how far they are true ? I know that Political Economy is called the dismal science. I know that it sounds wicked to put it before religion. But I don't mean wickedness, if you only knew my meaning. To me it would not be dismal, let it be never so dry and hard ; for it would tell me one thing, which I must be set at rest about before religion can ever tell me anything. And yet —it seems to me that language must all be wrong. It is religion—the very thing I am thinking about. It is part of it—it must be.'

'Go on,' said Mr. Stanley, 'tell me your meaning. Whatever it is, I am sure you don't mean wickedness. What is this that you wish to be set at rest about ?'

'Religion,' she said, 'you will, of course, tell me is the first thing. If I felt it was not I should be a bad Catholic. Well, what does Religion, what does the Church teach me ? Mr. Stanley, doesn't it teach me this—how to act under the circumstances in which I have been placed ? Of course it does : but the thing I want to know is, have I any right to remain under those circumstances ?'

'Go on,' said the priest. 'Don't be afraid of what you are thinking. Explain yourself a little more fully.'

She looked at him with a wistful inquiry,

something as a dog might. 'Are you under-standing me?' she said. 'Tell me. Or have I merely muddled myself with a dream? I am richer than other people. Have I any right to be so? Am I a robber—are we all of us robbers? Have we any business to be in the position we occupy? Oh, if you knew how, in some shape or other, some thought like this has been haunting me—I can't tell for how long! Often at balls last season I found myself thinking during supper of the hungry faces I had seen in the street outside. I once went over Mr. Snapper's manufactory, and watched the faces of the poor men working there. They no doubt had quite enough to eat; but in their looks, in their attitudes—I can see them at this moment—there seemed a reproach to me or a claim on me, I could not tell which. I have always felt when I heard of popular politics—and at home, as you know, we don't hear much, still we hear something—

I have always felt that there was something in the background which no one had the courage to recognize ; and now to-day I have heard it put into words.   When Mr. Foreman was talking, I couldn't understand it all ; but offensive as he was in many ways, and strange as his wording was to me, it somehow seemed to be what I had unconsciously been waiting for.   We are the cause, he said, we and the world we live in, of all the blight we see in the lives below us.   Is that so ?   Are we ?   We must know that—surely we must —before our minds can be satisfied.   Where does our duty lie—in which of these two opposite things—in renouncing our position or in using it ?   There, Mr. Stanley—I have spoken straight out now.   There is the question which seems to me, every day when I am saying my prayers, to come far before those questions which are commonly called religious. Am I wrong ?   Tell me if I am wrong.'

'My child,' he said, 'you are not. You are profoundly right. Political economy, and the social conditions of labour, have become in our day indeed a part of theology—its youngest branch ; and as such, I, a priest, have studied it. Yes, this question that troubles you is the one great question for those whose hearts God has moved to ask it. Every age has its riddle, and this riddle is ours. I, perhaps, may be able to give some help to you.'

'Oh,' she said quietly, ' but you have helped me already. I listened to every word you said this morning ; and I mainly understood Mr. Foreman from the way in which you argued with him. Oh, indeed you have helped me. Listen : the others are coming. I hear them in the wood under us. But before they come let me ask you one thing more. Let me say what I think you mean, and you tell me if I am correct.'

'Tell me,' he said. 'There is still time.'

'You don't believe, then, do you,' she said hurriedly, 'that all riches are robbery—that you and I, for instance, are living on stolen goods because we are staying at a castle—or because I give five shillings, say, for a pair of gloves ? You mean that the talents which produce money and so on—all those things that Mr. Foreman wishes to take from us—depend on the workings of our average human appetites ; that is to say, these talents would never be developed at all if it were not in the nature of things that those fortunate few who possess them, should possess also the riches which result from their exercise. Is not that what you mean ? '

'Exactly,' said Mr. Stanley. 'In considering human actions we must always remember this. The natural reward causes the effort, just as much as the effort wins the reward : and the Church, in its message to the world in general, never assumes for a moment that these natural rewards can be dispensed with. She enjoins not the extinction of the desire for them, but simply the regulation of it. The desire itself is presupposed as permanent. I am, of course, not speaking of the counsels of perfection.'

'No,' she said, 'but it was about those I was thinking.'

· 'You must remember,' he answered, 'that they, in their very nature, are addressed to a few only. They are plainly not addressed to a society as a society; for a society that followed them could not continue to exist.'

'Yes,' she said, 'but let us keep to the one matter we are talking about. Suppose all the men on whom the progress of industry depends had grace given them to forego the natural reward of their exertions—suppose they were still to make the same enormous profits, but instead of taking them, as they now do, for themselves, were to willingly hand them over for the general good—then there might be a state like that Mr. Foreman dreams about.   Is not that so ?'

'True,' said Mr. Stanley. 'But think of this.   Such a change must in its very nature be voluntary—more than voluntary : it must be enthusiastic.   It would have to come from the inner movements of men's spirits. We are little likely to see such a change as that.'

'Not in the world at large—no.   But it might—surely this is possible—take place in some.   Some might still make the exertion, develop all their faculties, and yet forego the natural reward.   They might extend commerce, they might develop manufactures, as if they were doing so under some monastic vow —some vow of poverty with a modern meaning in it.   It is at least conceivable that they might do so ; and if they did—well, I want to know, wouldn't they be doing good ?

'No doubt,' he said, 'if they acted thus they would.'

' Thank you,' she said; ' what I wished to ask you is answered.'

She rose from where she was sitting, and moved a few paces away from him ; and, looking down into the depths of the wood below, began to trifle with the grass that grew on a ruined parapet. She was standing thus when the rest of the party arrived ; and as she turned unwillingly round to confront them there was a curious something in her whole air and expression which caught, in an instant, Carew's experienced eye. 'If,' he exclaimed to himself, ' she had had any other companion, I should think she had just been listening to a declaration of love.' She, too, on her side, had seen the way in which he looked at her ; and though she had no time to inquire nicely into causes, she felt that for a second her heart beat quicker than usual. She felt, too, that she blushed ; and the blush was still on her cheeks when, a few moments later, history began to repeat itself, and Carew was again her companion on the way home.

'You seemed,' he said to her presently, 'to be having an interesting conversation just now, when we interrupted you.'

'When you came,' she said, 'I was not talking—I was thinking.'

'Will you tell me,' he asked, 'what your thoughts were? Were you thinking about what we heard this morning?'

'I was thinking,' she said, 'of something that will alter my whole life perhaps.' She stopped short abruptly, and walked on in silence, Carew meanwhile from time to time watching her. Presently she began again, taking up her former sentence, as if unconscious there had been any pause in her speaking. 'And yet,' she said, 'who can tell? Perhaps by next season I shall have forgotten all about it, and be thinking of nothing but balls and new ball-dresses. Do you think that's likely?' she went on, with a little nervous laugh. 'Or perhaps you don't know me well enough to be able to form an opinion.'

'I don't know,' said Carew, 'what it is you are speaking about; but about you I know, or at least believe, one thing. You will never be satisfied until you have seen the Right; and when you have seen it you will never be untrue to it. That is my belief about you; it is more than that—it is my faith.'

She looked up at him with a soft startled stare. 'Your faith about me!' she exclaimed. 'What grounds can you possibly have for a faith about me of that kind?'

'You yourself are the grounds,' he said. 'I know of none other. Do you remember yesterday, when you said something about the Mass, and I told you it shocked me? That was because of my faith in you. But this morning—you didn't see me—I was in chapel, though, watching you—this morning, the faith which you had shocked was much more than made whole again. I saw that the Mass was not to you what you said it was. It was not outside your inner life, but a part of it. Let me say to you just what I think. Let me think aloud to you, without either of us feeling embarrassed. Religion and faith are not things about which one pays silly compliments, and I am merely telling you what I mean and feel. It can do you no harm to hear it; perhaps it may do you good. Look at me,' he said, stopping in his walk suddenly; 'is the sun shining on my face, or do the trees hide it?'

' The sun shining on your face ? Yes—not in your eyes, but on your cheeks.'

'I couldn't have known that if you hadn't told me.'

'Naturally,' she said. 'You can't see your own face without a looking-glass.'

Carew suddenly turned to her with a look of earnestness. 'Then I could see,' he began, 'although you could not see——' But then his voice faltered. He lowered his eyes and he looked away from her.

'Tell me,' she said gently, 'what could you see?'

'I could see on your face and in your eyes this morning "The light that never was on sea or land." Come, let us move on.'

They resumed their walk in silence, which was for some time broken by nothing but an occasional sound of Carew's stick on a bramble. Presently, however, they emerged from a dense thicket, and the château all of a sudden came full into view before them, with its tower, its gardens, and its ramparts, crowning the hill opposite. There were some exclamations from both of them at the singular picturesqueness of the sight; and then Miss Consuelo turned to Carew and said, a trifle brusquely, ' You like to live in a castle, don't you ? '

' How do you mean ? ' he said.

' I mean, you like to lead a life that separates you not only from the vulgar rich—of course you like that—but from the common lot of men and women in general ? '

' For riches merely as riches,' replied Carew evasively, ' I care little or nothing. I would sooner eat a dinner of herbs with gentlemen than a stalled ox with people— well, with people of no family.'

' Yes, but if gentlemen are to hold their heads up in the world, there are certain surroundings which you think are due to them, to which morally they have a birth-right; and you yourself like to be sur-rounded by these. You would not like to renounce them?'

'To me,' he said, 'they are symbols—they are not luxuries.'

'What!' she exclaimed, suddenly bright-ening into a wayward laugh, 'do you lounge in a soft arm-chair to show the length of your pedigree?'

Carew laughed too; and until they reached the château the conversation lapsed into a less serious tone. Both, however, still were aware of serious thoughts beneath it; and when they were standing in the archway waiting for the others, Miss Consuelo again said in something of her former manner, 'Yes, this is the sort of thing you like—this stately seclusion, these battlements, these great coats-of-arms——'

'Well,' he said, 'and what are all these

but signs ?   Would you like yourself to renounce the thing they signify ?'

' No,' she said ; ' on that point I feel just as you do.   It is partly for what they signify that I would renounce the present signs.   I should find new ones.   What we have now I would sacrifice.'

' Tell me,' said Carew, ' what are the exact things you are thinking of.'

She looked at him as if she but half heard his question—as if her thoughts were wandering ; and her words, when she spoke, seemed little more than a ripple on the surface of a silent meditation.   ' Many things,' she said ; ' not only houses and lands and servants—other things, too—poetry, books, drawing,   self-development—perhaps   other things—all the unwritten poems of which one's own soul is the heroine.   I think all this is involved in the thought I have received to-day.   But I can't tell,' she said, rousing herself, 'I can't tell yet. That thought is like one of my own travelling-trunks. It will take a long time to unpack.'

'Will you not,' said Carew, 'let me help you in unpacking it ?'

'Perhaps some day,' she replied, 'perhaps never.' Then, with a little brusque movement of the head, she looked him in the eyes for a moment, and said, 'If anyone helps me, you shall.' The words were hardly uttered when a deep blush covered her cheeks, and changing her manner with a strong effort, she went on almost flippantly, 'But you wouldn't like the task. No, no ; these are the surroundings for you. You will live and die with liveried servants waiting on you. You are quite right about yourself. The people, for you, are dirt.'

'See,' said Carew, 'here come Lady Chislehurst and the others. I have something to say to them. Will you all of you,' he went on, 'come now with me, and I will show you what I said I would — how I occupy my solitude here. Perhaps,' and he turned again to Miss Consuelo Burton, ' you will find in this a reply to what you have just said.'

Carew led his guests, who were delighted at his proposal, into a side of the château which they had none of them yet visited ; and they presently entered a suite of small sitting-rooms, opening one into the other after the fashion of old houses.

' When,' he said, ' I was unpacking my books and papers, and wondering how on earth I should ever sort and arrange them, this little row of rooms struck me all at once as a godsend. I have consecrated one of them exclusively to each of my several tastes, or perhaps I should say more properly, of the several interests of my life. In this room — you see I have not used it much — in this room are all my poets, dramatists, novelists, and so on ; everything, in fact, that you call literature proper. Now come into the next. Here are all my books on philosophy and religion.'

' This room,' said Lady Chislehurst with approbation, ' looks more lived-in than the other. And—ah, I see you have all the great Catholic writers—nearly all are Catholic ; and here is Mr. Stanley's book on the life of the Angelical Doctor. But that table, Mr. Carew, has not been sat at lately ; or else your French housemaids are very bad hands at dusting.'

' Well,' said Carew, ' now come into the third room.'

An exclamation burst from several voices, and Harley said, expressing the meaning of all of them, ' Well now, Carew, we have got to your den at last.'

And a den indeed it was. Along the walls, on rudely constructed shelves, were rows upon rows of books, many of them bound in paper, whilst the floor was piled with reports and pamphlets, and official-looking folio-sheets covered with tabulated statistics. At each of the two windows there was, moreover, a writing-desk, and each of these desks was plainly in present use. The visitors slowly inspected the contents of the curiously unornamental library ; and volume after volume as they went the round of the room was seen directly or indirectly to deal with the same subject. Political Economy, and the social conditions of labour—the subject was that; the subject was that only. English, German, French and American manuals all were here; and still more numerous were rows of Reports and Blue-books.

'Here,' said Carew at last, 'is the scene of my daily life. My solitude is a nut, and here you get to the kernel of it. There is hardly a book, Mrs. Harley, of any present influence either in Europe or America, dealing with the labour question, or the land question, which I have not got here ; and I have also done my best to get all the most reliable accounts, official or otherwise, of the way the workers live in various countries, and their comparative comfort or misery at various periods. I am trying to reduce a number of my results to writing.'

'And who,' said Lady Chislehurst, 'sits at that other desk ? Do you keep an amanuensis ? '

' There he is,' said Carew, pointing to Mr. Stanley, ' or rather I am his. He this week is correcting, and I am helping him to correct, the proof-sheets of Mr. Griffen's work, which our poor friend Foreman was looking forward to as a new revelation. Now, Lady Chislehurst, I have made my confessions to our Society, as my contribution to its inaugural meeting.'

'I hope,' she said as they returned to the

room adjoining, 'that you've not abandoned this room—the room of your theologians.'

'At any rate,' said Carew, 'I have passed to the other through this; and to this, you see, I return, whenever I leave the other.'

Late in the evening, shortly before the party separated, he said in a low voice to Miss Consuelo Burton, 'And do you think that I care nothing about the people now?'

'No,' she replied, 'what I said I unsay.'

'And will you do this?' said Carew. 'One thing which you said—will you now say it over again? Will you say again, "If any one ever helps me, you shall "—will you say that?'

'Yes,' she murmured, 'I say it.'

That night, in her room, before she retired to bed, she opened a large despatch-box, and took out a number of papers from it. She put these before her on the writing-table, and she sat for a long time pensively looking over them. Her head rested on her hand as if wearily ; a half contemptuous smile flickered about her mouth; once or twice she gave a little cold soft laugh ; once or twice, too, a sigh escaped her. The papers were all in manuscript ; part was prose, part was verse. It was all of it her own composition. She had never shown it to any one, or ventured to hope that it could be of any value to others ; but it had been for her like a hidden store of honey, which she had secreted from time to time, obeying a natural impulse. To another reader she knew that the words might convey little ; but to her, when she wrote them, they were like so many constellations of stars, marking and fixing the figures created by her own imagination. In the case of the verse, it was the same, too, with regard to their melody. They were like notes in a copy of music, which only she could read, and which could be played only on the instrument of her own mind.

To-night they still charmed her, but not

as formerly. There was a difference. The thoughts, the sentiments, which it once so pleased her to chronicle, were now dear to her only as the toys of a lost childhood. With the mere melody it was otherwise. That, as she read, seemed sonorous and satisfying as ever. It was as though she were herself singing to herself, and she turned the pages regretfully as if the sound fascinated her. But no sooner had she come to the last page than, rising from her seat, she gathered them all together, and then, moving towards the chimney, carefully placed them across the iron dogs and set fire to them. She stood looking at them, as a mother might look at a dead child, whilst they burned slowly. Then, when the last blue flames were flickering faint amongst the folded embers, she pressed her hands tightly across her eyes ; her lips quivered a little, and she murmured half aloud, 'What is poetry or the poetry of life to me!'

Lord Aiden and Carew, on the terrace just below her, were meanwhile pacing up and down together, smoking their cigarettes, whilst the stars glittered above them. Lord Aiden, who, in spite of his dilettante languor, was really touched by poetry more deeply than by anything, and had always escaped to it as a refuge from imperial politics and diplomacy, repeated in Greek that loveliest of all Greek epigrams, of which the following is a widely-known translation—

> My love, thou gazest on the skies :
>   Ah, would that I might be
> Those skies, with all their thousand eyes,
>   That I might gaze at thee !

'We were talking the other night,' he went on, 'about the inversion of similes. I have often thought that we might invert the whole thought of that poem. Some men are constant not to a woman but womanhood, and instead of seeing in the skies an image of themselves as they would wish to be, they see in them the image of womanhood as it actually is.   They do not wish for a thousand eyes to look at any one woman ; but they see the same mysterious inexhaustible charm of womanhood everywhere looking out of a thousand eyes at them.   They are pantheists in love, and they are not inconstant though they seem to be.'

' I,' said Carew, ' hitherto have been a pantheist somewhat of that kind ; but no woman could ever move me now, unless we both clung together to a something beyond ourselves.'

BOOK III.

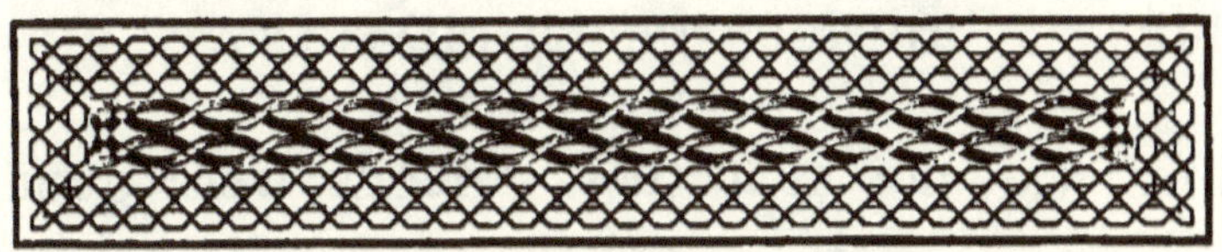

CHAPTER I.

 FEW days later, the château was dull and silent ; and Carew once more was alone in it. Indoors, on his desk, his books and papers invited him ; outside, the sun was shining brightly as ever : but nothing pleased or satisfied him as it had done formerly. It is not surprising, when a house has been full of guests, if the host who remains behind should feel depressed by the solitude ; but Carew's depression did not arise from this. The mere absence of his friends he could have borne with perfect composure ; and the thing that weighed upon

him was not that these friends were gone, but the peculiar circumstances which had attended the going of one of them.

On Sunday night he had persuaded the whole party to stay on with him at least till Tuesday ; and Monday was to be occupied in some picturesque excursion, a prospect which filled Miss Consuelo Burton with pleasure.

But on Monday morning, soon after the post arrived, Mrs. Harley had come to him with an odd look in her face, and informed him, in a manner not far from embarrassment, that she had just had a letter from the eldest Miss Burton.

'Who has been telling her things?' said Mrs. Harley. 'I am sure I don't know ; but she has heard already—she must have heard it yesterday—that Consuelo has been meeting Foreman here. She is very much annoyed about it, and wishes her to come back imme- diately. Consuelo, poor child, has had a letter from her, too. She won't show it to me ; but I can see it is disagreeable. Has Elfrida not written to you ?'

Carew drew from his pocket a number of unopened envelopes. 'I will look,' he said. ' Yes, this must be hers.'

It was a note couched in the coldest terms of civility. ' When I allowed my sister,' it said, ' to come to your house, I did so believing that she would be safe from meeting a person whose opinions and character are notoriously offensive to her family, and with whom they could never allow her to associate for an instant. Since this, however, proves not to have been the case, it will hardly surprise you that I have asked Mrs. Harley to arrange for my sister's return at the earliest moment possible ; and we are sending a carriage to fetch her, which, so far as we can ascertain, will arrive at your house very nearly as soon as this letter.'

'I can never,' said Mrs. Harley, 'let her go back alone. I am more sorry than I can say to leave you in this way. George, of course, can remain; but I, you will see yourself, must really go back with her; and I have no doubt that the moment I see Elfrida I shall be able to show her that you have been not to blame.'

To this Carew could offer no opposition; indeed, annoyed as he was at the whole incident, what he felt most was the position of Miss Consuelo herself. 'Where is she?' he asked Mrs. Harley. 'I should like to speak to her.'

'She is in her room,' said Mrs. Harley, 'getting ready to start; and I must go too. Poor child, she is painfully troubled; and the instant the carriage comes she begged we might be off. For aught I know, it may be here already.'

He saw neither of the two ladies again

till a minute or two before their departure. He had no opportunity of saying one word to Miss Consuelo privately ; and indeed, till he was actually seeing them into the carriage he was unable to do as much as catch her eye for a moment. At last he did this in the act of saying ' Good-bye ' to her ; and what was his sensation then ? What emotions were they that he read in the look she turned on him ? Was sympathy there ? Was there any feeling of friendliness ? To his surprise, there was nothing but a frigid stare of indifference ; and when he proceeded, before his surprise had overpowered him, to murmur some hope of their very soon meeting again, she merely replied with a civil conventional little laugh, ' I'm rather afraid we are going to leave Nice presently.'

As to the question of Foreman, he talked that over with Mr. Stanley, and he had little doubt that that would be soon explained.   He wrote Miss Burton a letter about it ; and felt fully able to clear himself. On that score he was soon at ease.   But his mind was full of some dim foreboding consciousness that there was something behind, which he had not yet arrived at ; and all through the time that the rest of his friends remained with him, he was haunted and stung by the thought of this unexplained parting.   The day after it, he had sent Miss Consuelo a line or two, to say simply how he hoped he had not offended her ; and now that his guests were gone, and there was nothing whatever to distract him, he was pacing after breakfast up and down the ramparts, wondering if the post would bring him any, or what, answer.

Absorbing, however, as this thought was, it left room in his mind for others of a more important nature ; indeed the excitement caused by it seemed to compel their presence.

His old desponding impression that the existing social world, with its soil of centuries, in which all his life was rooted, and with which alone he could conceive himself as having any relations—his impression that this world was on the eve of its destruction, and that the very ground he trod on was slipping away under his feet, returned to him more vivid than ever. The stately hush of the old halls and parks, which represented to him the climate in which his own thoughts had grown, and out of which he could hardly think at all, he seemed to see invaded by two discordant armies—a savage mad proletariat armed with axes and firebands, and an impertinent middle-class entrenching itself in villas, and devastating the aristocratic solitudes with sandwich-papers and the claws of lobsters. This impression was again traversed by another, that matters were not yet hopeless; and that though it was a riddle how to save what he clung to, the riddle had an answer, if he only knew where to find it. But both his hope and his despondency, and all the care included in them, were, for the time being, inseparable from the thought of Miss Consuelo Burton. *They* seemed like emanations from *it; it* seemed perpetually to be shaping itself out of *them*.

Such was his mood of mind when the stable-clock struck ten—the hour when the post was due: and before long a tray of letters was brought to him. He had only expected one which could bear on his anxiety. Instead of one there were three. There was the one he expected; he knew it must be her handwriting; he looked at the back, and there he saw her monogram. Besides that there was one from her eldest sister, and there was another from Mrs. Harley.

He read the one from the eldest sister first. She accepted Carew's explanation with regard to the presence of Foreman, but she did so in phrases of such studied coldness as to show that her displeasure remained, although the alleged pretext for it had been abandoned. This was apparent in even the first few sentences ; and then followed something that was even more unequivocal. 'My sister has received the note which you thought fit to address to her on this subject, and with my sanction is herself writing to inform you that she is perfectly satisfied with your explanations. We must beg, therefore, that you will not put yourself to the trouble of either thinking or writing any more about it.'

He crushed the letter in his hand with a sense of anger and perplexity ; and it was some time before he looked at the others. He resumed his walk at a more rapid pace, the very stamp of his feet betraying the mood that possessed him : and it was not till he had several times been the whole length of the ramparts that he found himself prepared to open Miss Consuelo's envelope.   Within its folds there was still some faint hope for him, but so faint that, like a flickering candle, it produced not light so much as an instant fear of darkness.   At last, however, he tore it open and faced the contents.   In a second his hope had vanished.   Her few lines were as follows :

'DEAR MR. CAREW,—Your letter told me nothing that I had not already known.   I was much interested in meeting Mr. Foreman ; but the incident, which you may have surmised would be very displeasing to my relations, was, so far as you are concerned, not only accidental but unavoidable : and I can assure you they are now quite aware of the fact.   I am glad to have an opportunity of thanking you for my interesting visit ; and also of telling you that, everything being perfectly clear, no further explanations of any kind are necessary.

'I am, yours truly,

'C. Burton.'

This letter he crushed even more violently than the other. He seemed for the moment to be on the point of tearing it up; but changed his mind, and thrust it angrily into his pocket. Mrs. Harley's still remained for him; he felt, however, that that might keep; he had read quite enough for the present. He went indoors, put on a stout pair of walking-shoes, and, letting it be known that he would not be in till the evening, resolved to seek consolation in a long excursion on foot.

However heavily trouble may weigh upon one, there is a comfortless exhilaration in the effort to shake it off; and Carew, when he emerged again, felt that his spirits rose a little. The charms of the day and country had also something to do with this. Colour and sunlight had naturally upon him much the same effect that music has upon some people ; and sore with a sense of undeserved injury, he yielded himself now to their blandishments with a kind of defiant recklessness. The blinding blue of the sky, the liquid luxurious atmosphere which made the whole panorama glitter as if it were seen through water, the tints of the hills and hollows, the golden flash of the oranges, and the misty bloom of azure which slept on the distant mountains, and seemed as one looked to palpitate with its own intensity —all this struck on Carew's nerves like the crash of some inspiriting orchestra. In a half-hearted way it made him feel a man again. Where he would go he had not yet decided ; but his eyes fell suddenly on a little mediæval town, shining over its olive-yards far off in the upland country. He had often heard reports of it—of its towers, its fortifications, and its singular antique houses. This was Saint Paul du Var. He resolved that he would go there now.

The walk was lovely. The country as he went revealed to him, by road or mule-path, its quaintest scenes and the choicest of its secret prospects; and at last, after three hours' travel, on emerging from a grove of cork-trees, he saw on the opposite side of a deep but narrow gully, a glimmering girdle of grey walls and bastions; above these, a huddling cluster of windows, roofs, and balconies, and crowning all, a church and a square watch-tower.

Continuing to follow the pathway which had brought him thus far, he arrived in the course of five or ten minutes more at a wooded slope, which shelved down to a carriage-road, or rather a space in which the carriage-road ended; and on the farther side of this was the embattled gate of the town.

Here he paused ; and seeing that the ground was inviting, he sat down on the dry brown pine-needles, and drew from his pocket some slight luncheon he had brought with him. Despite his unhappiness exercise had made him hungry ; and as he ate a reflective calm stole over him, such as often accompanies the satisfaction of any natural craving. He looked at the scene before him with a quiet dejected interest. It was full of sympathetic suggestions. The narrow gateway that confronted him, flanked by two mouldering towers ; the walls, pierced with loopholes, that ran to left and right of it, were still nearly as perfect as when their builders had left them. Little had changed them but the noiseless action of time, which had laid on them the tints of centuries. Close by these walls were several rude carts, plainly too wide to pass through the narrow arch. In and out amongst them were some little children playing ; an old crone with a distaff sat in the sunshine watching them ; and some twenty yards away a bevy.of laughing girls were grouped together round a bubbling marble conduit, and with quick brown arms were washing their store of linen. Then presently there was a slight noise behind him. He turned to look, and straying downwards from the forest a boy goat-herd, actually playing on a pipe, passed by with his goats, like a figure out of a story-book.

Carew, as he sat contemplating this idyllic picture, instead of forgetting his own personal trouble, felt it by contrast assuming a clearer shape. For a second time in his life, Miss Consuelo Burton was lost to him ; but the circumstances now made the loss more crushing than formerly. Then she had left him against her will, and regretfully. Now she took part with those who told her to turn her back upon him. And why ? for what reason ? All the sins of his life rose up before him, as

they are said to do before the eyes of a drown-
ing man.   At first he accused himself, and
said with a bitter humility, 'I am an unclean
man.   She is quite right in departing from
me.'   Then he compared—he could not help
doing so—his own life with the lives of certain
other men whom he knew the Miss Burtons
treated with marked favour ; and in what
way, he wondered, could he be worse than
these ?   And why was he worse to-day than
he had been a week before ?   Miss Consuelo
was lost to him : that was one pain.   But
this, for the time being, was almost lost in
another.   He felt not as if he had been
wounded, but as if he had been beaten all
over ; and he was conscious of a sense of
blank and wondering desolation, out of which
affection had disappeared like a trampled
plant.   All the present seemed somehow pitted
against him.   It was as hard and unjust to
him, in the person of his private acquaint-

ances, as it was alien to him in its general social tendencies ; and the past, embodied in the objects now surrounding him, seemed to be receiving and soothing him like a tender personal friend.

He rose presently and entered the little town. He wandered eagerly through its narrow winding streets, noting with keen glance every detail of interest—the decayed scutcheon over a door that had once been noble ; the rich ironwork of some mediæval balcony ; or a well glimmering in the middle of some court-yard, its marble rim gashed with deep notches by the rope that had raised for centuries its still luminous water. At last a crooked alley brought him out upon the ramparts, and, having looked about him for a few minutes, he sat down on an old rusty cannon, which had probably lain where it was unmoved since the days of Vauban. Everything his eye fell on harmonized with his own spirit.

The old masonry, the fortifications, the immemorial houses, in their forlorn survival, and in their utter absence of hope, seemed, as it were, to be a part of his own being.

In this mood of mind he bethought himself of Mrs. Harley's letter. He could learn nothing from it that would add to his unhappiness ; it might contain something that would at least ease his anxiety. It began, as might have been expected, with a number of civil things about the charms of Courbon-Loubet, and the unpleasantness of Miss Consuelo's departure. It then went on to repeat the assurances which Carew had received already from two other quarters, and which added to his uneasiness rather than took away from it—that the Burtons, so far as Foreman's presence was concerned, now realized fully that they had no complaint against him. The letter went on as follows :

' You know, however, what Elfrida is ;

and somehow or other, there has been some mischief made about you. What it exactly means I really can't make out ; but I think I have gathered one thing—that that insufferable Mr. Inigo is at the bottom of it. Perhaps that may tell you something. It doesn't tell me much ; and Elfrida is as close as her own father confessor, and when she is opinionated there is no one so perverse as she is. I should like to shake her. However, these little matters, though they are very annoying at the time, soon blow over and clear themselves up, if one only lets them alone. Indeed, my dear Mr. Carew, if I had nothing to tell you but this it would hardly have been worth while for me to inflict a letter on you. But I have more to tell you than this.

' Here, then, is some news which you may not yet have seen in the papers : indeed parts of it have only just reached me by a private telegram. Here is some news which will at once amuse and please you. Eighteen out of twenty of our friend Foreman's elections have come off already. Eighteen of his Socialist candidates, who were to rally round them, in all its terrible strength, the voting force of educated and of organized labour—Foreman thought that the result would make all England tremble, probably all Europe—well, of these eighteen gentlemen, the one who polled most votes polled—how many should you think ? Out of eight thousand votes, and in a constituency supposed to be the most revolutionary in the kingdom, this terrible candidate polled a hundred and ninety-five ; and none of the other eighteen polled as many as thirty. Poor Foreman ! It's impossible not to pity him ; and yet, though I like him, it's impossible not to be amused at him. You never saw a man so completely knocked down in your life. I dare say in a week or two he'll be full of explanations, but he hasn't had time

to think of *one* yet. He's positively as white
as a sheet, except when I make fun of him,
and then he gets red with anger—or rather he
did; for, I believe to avoid me, he has gone
off to spend a week in retreat at Mentone;
and from thence, he told me, he is going
back straight to London. There was something almost ghastly in the eyes of the poor
creature when he warned me at parting that
we should soon hear again of him, and that
his members without constituencies—I don't
know how they'll manage—will soon hold a
Parliament that will make us all tremble, in
the streets. Meanwhile, I think you and I
may congratulate ourselves that the old order
of things has still got legs to stand upon
—even, perhaps, the old families with their
quarterings. Only, you and your friends must
show them how to be useful; and—a thing
which is even more important—you must get
them to be so after you have shown them.

'The Burtons leave Nice to-morrow for Rome, where they remain till Easter, and where we expect to join them, and then we talk of going home together by the Italian lakes. I wish there was any chance of your being at your cousin's beautiful island villa at that time, and that we might all meet again. I have not the least doubt that between this and then Elfrida will have unbosomed her secret to me ; and I shall be able to show her what a ridiculous mare's-nest it has been. Yes—depend upon it : like a good soul as she is, in another three weeks she will be humbly begging your pardon, and you will be generously dissembling your sense that she looks foolish.'

The first part of the letter told Carew little. The mention, indeed, of Mr. Inigo's name produced a passing emotion of contemptuous and irritated wonder ; but what Mrs. Harley said with regard to the Burtons merely deepened his blank and almost dreamlike sense of estrangement from them. The elder sisters, he felt, might believe or disbelieve what they pleased; but nothing could soften his memory of the way in which the younger one had parted from him. Very different was the effect of the political news that had reached him. The vast forces of change which were supposed to be undermining society, and which seemed to menace with their widespread and subterranean rumblings the imminent ruin of all the existing fabric—these forces had put their strength to the test : and with what result ? The terrible Titan, so it seemed to Carew, had shrunk to the proportions of a squalid malignant dwarf. He felt like a man relieved suddenly from a nightmare. He was not in a mood to criticise this impression. It came to him by surprise ; he received it glowing with gratitude ; and a sense of exhilaration spread itself through all his body, as if after a long fast he had drunk some strong stimulant.

He rose from his seat. The Château de Courbon-Loubet, seem to rear itself on its hill with a bolder and statelier dignity. The old buildings round him partook of the same spirit. They ceased to look forlorn; they defied change and progress. He resumed his walk with a light and excited step, resolving to see, if possible, the interiors of some of the houses. Full of these thoughts, he was descending a flight of steps which led down from the ramparts to the level of the ground below, when his foot slipped and he found that he had sprained his ankle. The immediate pain was not great, but he feared that it would soon increase, and he was at once confronted with a doubt as to how he should get home.

The scene of the accident was close to the gateway of the town, and, recollecting the carts he had noticed outside, he made his way to them limping, in order to see if he could not engage one as a vehicle. He had hardly, however, emerged from the shadow of the arch, when the first sight that presented itself was a carriage, which must have arrived lately. The horses had been taken out, but the coachman was in his place on the box, and was placidly regaling himself with the contents of some paper packages. Carew's ankle at the moment beginning to be more painful, his ordinary scruples at once went to the winds; and he inquired with interest of the coachman from what place he had come, and of what his party consisted. The carriage had come from Cannes; its occupants were three people, and they were now inspecting the town. Carew, on hearing this, explained his condition to the coachman; told him he was anxious to get to the Château de Courbon-Loubet, which lay hardly more than a mile off the direct Cannes road; and then, with the present of a five-franc piece, begged him to look for his employers, and ask them if, of their goodness, they would give a lift to a gentleman who had just lamed himself.

But he had hardly finished speaking when the coachman, with a jerk of his thumb, exclaimed, ' Voilà, monsieur!' and Carew, turning his head, saw coming towards him the very people in question. There was a tall bronzed man, with a somewhat military bearing, walking slowly by the side of a middle-aged lady—a lady whose face was singularly gentle in expression, and who was a little singular too, for the richness of her Parisian dress. There was something in her look and movements so attractive and soothing, that Carew had hardly time to do more than notice that a second lady of some sort was walking a short way behind them, under the shade of a fanciful brown parasol : and he was just preparing, though not without some shyness, to advance and meet the two foremost of the strangers, when their companion, moving her parasol, caught sight of him and started. He started also. They both had a second look at each other; and Carew recognized in the strangers Miss Capel and her parents.

The girl's smile had still the same charm for him, the same frankness, the same tantalizing mystery, that it had had on the mountain road and in the moonlit garden at Nice. With a quick elastic step she came forward to meet him; and a welcome in her eyes flashed like sunshine on trembling water. He too moved forward a step or two. There was something intoxicating in the pleasure she showed at seeing him; and he hardly knew whether his ankle pained him or no.

'Mamma,' she said, 'this is Mr. Carew, who saved my precious fan for me—the beautiful one you gave me. Mr. Carew, this is General Capel.'

'You seem,' said Mrs. Capel, 'to have much the same tastes as we have. We are devoted to wanderings amongst these old places.'

'But, God bless my soul!' exclaimed the General, 'have you hurt yourself? You seem as if you could hardly walk.'

Carew explained that such was indeed the case, and that when they appeared he was just nerving himself to ask if they would take him home in their carriage.

'I discovered,' he said, 'from your coachman that you had come from Cannes—I see you have left Nice—and my house lies almost directly upon the way.'

'And how have you come?' inquired Mrs. Capel kindly. 'Have you walked?'

Carew explained that he had, and also where he was living.

'I remember,' the girl exclaimed, 'you told me you had a castle somewhere. Fancy a castle in these days ! You are like a prince out of a fairy-tale.'

'Mr. Carew,' interposed Mrs. Capel, 'I am forgetting myself. We are letting you stand when you ought to be sitting down. Come, get into the carriage, and make yourself comfortable. The back seat—I insist. I'm accustomed to be obeyed in these things. That's right, and like a sensible person. And now, if you'll take my advice, rest your foot on the seat opposite.'

Mrs. Capel's voice was unusually soft and musical, and there was a trace in her of that simple and yet most dangerous charm which, Carew was already aware, was one of her daughter's attributes. The child-like, the unconscious, the fearless frankness of manner, though never more familiar than that of a well-bred friend, was wholly without the ceremonious distance found and expected in an ordinary well-bred acquaintance : and the impression produced on Carew, both by mother and daughter, was peculiar. It was not as if they had pushed themselves with any effort into his confidence ; but as if without effort, like two witches or fairies, they had traversed the space by which mundane strangers are separated, and put themselves noiselessly close to him by a mere act of sympathy.

Mrs. Capel's commands as a nurse he found there was no resisting. He arranged himself exactly in the attitude she suggested ; and then the daughter, with a smile of mimic authority, got into the carriage and propped his back up with a cushion.

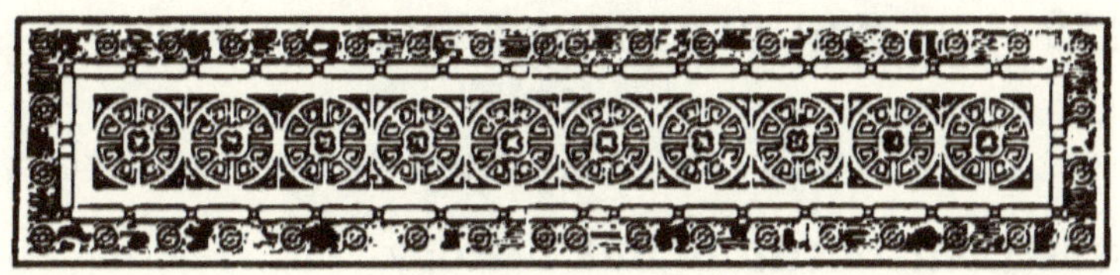

CHAPTER II.

URING the earlier part of the drive, so
far as Miss Capel was concerned, it
was enough for Carew to be pleasantly conscious that she was there. Her
pretty jacket, her black hat trimmed with
honeysuckle, her light brown gloves, and her
pocket-handkerchief edged with forget-me-
nots, all combined to make up a piquant
picture, which took a meaning from the sense
that her eyes were watching him. But his
whole conversation he gave to the two elders,
anxious to arrive at some sort of conclusion

as to who and whence they were and what was their position and history.

He gradually learnt quite enough to transform them from social phantoms into flesh-and-blood social realities. The General, who spoke with a slightly un-English accent, was descended not remotely from a well-known English family ; his parents, however, had settled in the Southern States of America, and his military rank was that of an officer in the Confederate army. As to Mrs. Capel he could not glean quite so much ; but he gathered from something said that she too was a Southerner by birth, though the greater part of her life had been passed in Paris and London. In addition to this, though there was no trace in her manner of any desire to boast of any great acquaintances, she betrayed quite accidentally that she had one or two intimate friends, amongst not only men but women, of the highest position and character.

It is true that there breathed about her a certain perfume of Bohemia, but it was a Bohe-
mian perfume of the highest and most delicate
kind.

By-and-by, having talked with the parents
enough to establish for them and himself some
mutual social footing, he began to address
himself more particularly to the daughter ;
nor was he long in discovering at least one
new charm in her. This was her keen sense
of the beauty of the scenes around her. She
not only saw but felt it ; and in the little remarks which she made from time to time on
the changing effects of shadow and light and
colour, still more in the pensive silence in
which she would sometimes watch them, he
felt, as it were, that he was listening to a
musical instrument, from which the outer
world was eliciting some tender delightful
melody. In the radiant morning, as he started
for his walk, nature had appealed to him

directly ; now it appealed to him through the appeal it made to a woman, and came fraught with the music and mystery of a woman's heart. The imaginative impression that he was listening to some actual tune grew on him with a dreamy enchantment ; but its meaning, as he listened to it, became more and more ambiguous. Now it was a woman's longing for a love that had not yet come to her ; now it was a woman's regret for some dead love or lover ; now it was the sound of a child singing one of Blake's ' Songs of Innocence.'

Meanwhile the afternoon was waning : the sunlight first grew rich with a warm gold colour ; then into this came a stealthy flush of rosiness ; and by-and-by the west was barred with crimson ; and the purple dusk of the twilight descended from the stainless sky.

Miss Capel looked round her as the silent darkness deepened ; and, after a long pause, murmured almost in a whisper, ' The shadows seem to fall on everything, just as the dew does.' There was a spell as she spoke, not in the words so much as in the tone. The tone seemed to say, as distinctly as any language could, that it came from a heart which would not be so touched now if it were not tender for very different causes, or at least if it would not be.

' Look,' said Carew, as a turn of the road brought into view a new reach of country, ' there is the château at the top of the further hill.'

' Indeed!' said the General. ' It must be a very interesting place. I was wondering what it was as we came along this morning.'

' And I hope,' said Mrs. Capel, ' as soon as you get there, Mr. Carew, you will be careful of that ankle of yours. Will you let us send over a doctor from Cannes to you?

We are quite early : you needn't look at your watch.'

' I was looking at my watch,' said Carew, ' not with any thought of the doctor, but because I wanted to ask you if you would remain and dine with me.'

' I am afraid,' said Mrs. Capel, ' that it's too late for that.'

' No,' retorted Carew, laughing ; ' I'm not going to let you off. It's too late for one thing—for you to make that excuse. Let us ask the General.' The General politely hesitated. ' And you, Miss Capel,' Carew went on, ' what do you say ? Would you like the arrangement ? ' Miss Capel said nothing, but with a soft, almost solemn smile, raised her eyes to his and nodded her head slowly. They at once moved in a world of secret mutual understanding.

' Come,' Carew resumed, ' let us consider that that is settled. Your horses will be all the better for resting; and you, Mrs. Capel, who have been so kind to me as an invalid, must know that for a sufferer there is nothing like pleasant company.'

These persuasions were, before long, successful; and it was quite evident that the Capels were pleased to have been persuaded. Little had Carew expected when he set forth in the morning, desolate and depressed about everything—about life and love and politics—little had he expected that he should return a few hours later with an excitement that disguised if it did not cure his unhappiness. And yet such was, indeed, the case. Only for one moment, as they crossed, in nearing the château, the track of his Sunday walk with Miss Consuelo Burton, did a sickening pain, a despairing regret come back to him. But it passed presently; the remarks of his new friends drowned it; and in the pleasure

N

and expectation they betrayed as the five-sided tower drew nearer, he felt a renewal of his own fresh sensations on perceiving it first himself. Indeed, when they arrived at the great arched entrance, and he conducted his guests across the court into the interior, he was conscious of an excitement, in receiving these chance strangers, which last week had been altogether wanting when he was performing the same office to his friends. To his friends the château had appealed as a fragment of history—as part of a past to which they had some close relation. To his present guests it was a fragment, not of history, but of fairyland. It was a delightful adventure to them to find themselves in the midst of it; and to him by sympathy it became an adventure also. Everything suddenly acquired the charm of strangeness. The table covered with its familiar glass and silver, and the faded liveries of the lackeys dimly moving in the background—he could hardly believe that he had ever seen any of it before.

'I wish,' he said as dinner drew to an end, 'that I could take you for a walk on the terrace and through the gardens in the moonlight.'

'No, no,' said Mrs. Capel, 'you keep yourself quiet. There was an arm-chair in the room where we were just now, which I at once took note of as the very thing for an invalid. Perhaps the General and Violet might go out and look about them for a moment; and meanwhile, I will give you a little medical advice.'

Carew was not pleased exactly at the notion of being parted from Miss Capel; but Mrs. Capel, by some mysterious exercise of authority, contrived, when they rose from the table and passed into the adjoining salon, that her husband and daughter should do as she had suggested; and she herself and Carew were presently left together. He soon comprehended the reason of this gentle and adroit manœuvre.

With a kind imperiousness she saw him arranged in comfort; and then, with a grave expression, taking a seat close to him, 'I had heard from my daughter,' she said, 'how you had met her at Madame de Saint Valery's —Madame de Saint Valery is, as you know, my niece. What a sad story hers is!'

'It is,' said Carew. 'No one knows that better than I do. There was never a woman who had more good in her——'

'Yes, yes,' said Mrs. Capel, interrupting him, 'and never a woman who has come to greater evil. Mr. Carew,' she continued, 'you have never before heard of me; but though I never expected to see you, I have heard a good deal of you. I know how on the night before she finally threw over everything, you took her for a walk by the side of the river at Hurlingham, and made her tell you the trouble that you saw was on her mind. I know how she told you plainly the desperate resolve she had taken, and how you did all you could to dissuade her. Her husband was in St. Petersburg. He had never behaved well to her. In all London she had no real friend but you; and you, though people said you were yourself in love with her, did all you could, like a real friend, to save her. Mr. Carew, I know it was from no selfish motive. You were no rival of the man who did the mischief. You wonder how I know. My unhappy niece has told me.'

'If ever I,' said Carew, 'had any influence for good on her, it was only because in herself there was so much goodness naturally.'

'There was,' said Mrs. Capel; 'and it was for this reason that I allowed Violet the other night to go to her. But—I hoped for an opportunity of speaking to you on this subject—*that* can never occur again. I suppose you are hardly aware what has happened to that poor creature by this time. She is now with some Russian prince—a real prince, but a ruined man and a thorough-paced scoundrel. She is with this man,' said Mrs. Capel, drawing closer to Carew, and lowering her voice, though there was no one at hand to overhear her, 'and she helps him in keeping a private gambling-hell at Nice. The whole thing is done with the utmost secrecy. Their great effort is to elude the vigilance of the police. It seems there is a club of them, and they meet in different houses—never at the same house two nights running. Can you fancy anything more dreadful ? Any morning we may see in the papers that she has been arrested. This is the reason why we have left Nice. It is a sad story, but I wished to tell it you ; partly because you had taken an interest in her, and partly because I wished to explain to you how my child came to be with her. That was a circumstance which otherwise you might have easily misunderstood.'

'No,' said Carew, 'I think not. At all events, I understand it perfectly now. Poor Madame de Saint Valery; fancy her having come to that!'

'Isn't it extraordinary!' said Mrs. Capel. 'And it's not for the sake of money that she has formed her present connection. She has money of her own—plenty of it. She has just bought a villa in Italy. No—it's simply an impulse, a caprice for this man; but a caprice, while it lasts, as generous as the best kind of affection. Yes, Mr. Carew, hers is a fine nature ruined.'

Whilst she was speaking servants appeared with coffee.

'And now,' she went on, 'let us send for

them to come in from the terrace. Perhaps also you will allow me to order the carriage.'

'Not yet,' said Carew ; 'you can wait half an hour longer. Think when you are gone how lonely and desolate I shall feel.'

'Mr. Carew,' said Miss Capel, appearing at the window, 'this is the most beautiful place, I think, I ever saw in my life. Can we ever thank you enough for having let us see it ?'

'Yes, you can,' said Carew ; and then turning to Mrs. Capel, 'you can thank me easily,' he added, 'in one way ; and in one way only. Come here again, and pay me a visit for a day or two. I am quite alone here ; and, as you know, I am partly crippled. But I could at least show you some of the neigh-bourhood, which is beautiful ; and if you were not afraid of finding the place dull, you would certainly prevent its being exceedingly dull to me.'

There was a little pause, and Mrs. Capel looked at her husband. 'I am afraid,' said Carew, 'that the General would not find much to amuse him.'

'Oh, it's not that,' said Mrs. Capel. 'The General at the present moment likes quiet better than anything. He's writing an account of the Battle of Bull Run for one of the New York magazines. To us, I am sure, nothing could be more delightful.'

'Then in that case,' said Carew, 'we will consider the matter settled. It only remains for us to fix the day.'

'I'm afraid,' said the General, 'it can't be till the week after next. Next week we are obliged to go to Genoa.'

'Then why not this week?' said Carew. 'Have you any engagements this week?' It appeared that they had not. Carew's heart beat with pleasure. 'Well, then,' he said, 'suppose that you come to-morrow. To-morrow is Thursday. That would give you a few days here, at any rate.'

Again there was some hesitation, and a little family council ; but the result was quickly arrived at, and after one or two rapid arguments, the invitation was accepted with the prettiest grace in the world.

CHAPTER III.

THE Capels, when they went—when their carriage disappeared into the darkness, seemed to Carew to have come and gone like a vision, and all his cares crowded back again on him. The vacant rooms were again filled with his friends; he heard the voices that echoed his own feelings ; the chairs, the walls, all the objects around him, told him that the eyes of Miss Consuelo Burton had rested on them : and he asked himself in a fit of weary and useless repentance why he had invited these strangers to profane and trouble his solitude. He remained in this mood during most of the next day, and had hardly tried to get free of it before his visitors came.   When he thought of the girl who had so readily charmed him yesterday, another image like a ghost revealed itself by the side of hers, and hers became almost an annoyance, which disturbed without distracting him.

Luckily, however, for the credit of his own civility, the Capels' actual arrival roused a little of his yesterday's interest in them, and, helped by a crutch, he limped out to welcome them.   There they were with a cortège of two carriages, one containing themselves, the other their boxes and servants. The moment he saw them again he felt his pulse quicken, and a number of minute impressions were stamped upon his memory in a moment—the spiked moustache and brown hands of the General, the dove-like glance and the delicately faded face of the mother, and the dainty audacity, almost too much like that of a fashion-book, which caught his eye in Miss Capel's dress as she descended.

Then followed presently the same little round of incidents which had marked the arrival of the Harleys and Miss Consuelo Burton. There was the same gathering in another ten minutes round the tea-table; there was the very same tea-service. But the room, and everything in it, though nothing whatever had been changed, was like the same instrument having a new tune played on it, and it seemed to be filled with a wholly different atmosphere.

Mrs. Capel's eye at once lit on the cups; and drawing off a long grey glove, which she extracted with difficulty from under a heavy bracelet, she took one of them up and examined it with the air of a connoisseur. 'Do you know,' she exclaimed, 'that these are perfectly priceless!' And she informed Carew of their exact date and history. Soon after she was attracted by the old silver tea-pot, and

she seemed equally able to give an opinion
about that.

'This old place,' she said, looking round
her with a smile of soft surprise, 'must
be a regular museum if all of it is like
this room. Do you see, Violet, those fiddles
and flutes over the door there? They are
exactly like what the Count has at Saint
Cloud in his billiard-room. You must
know, Mr. Carew, that I am devoted to
china and *bric-à-brac*. We have a house at
Saint Cloud ourselves ; and our neigh-
bour, whom I was just speaking of, is one
of the greatest collectors in Paris. Are
you,' she added, again looking at the tea-
cups, 'are you very fond of these beautiful
things yourself ?'

'I like them here,' said Carew, 'because
they are in keeping with the place.'

Mrs. Capel, however, hardly heard this,
for, looking up, she exclaimed with enthu-

siasm, 'What a pity it is that they should be all thrown away here ! For your cousin, I think you told me, never comes here himself; and your presence is nothing more than an accident. However, as it's not your house, I am going to indulge my feelings, and admire, and admire, and admire everything to my heart's content. Rudolph,' she went on to her husband, 'look at these lovely curtains. They're exactly like that brocade on the walls of Violet's sitting-room.'

Carew felt suddenly that he began to understand something as to where the difference lay between his new friends and himself. The contents of the château pleased and satisfied him because to him they were the right things in the right place; they delighted, but they surprised, Mrs. Capel because they were the right things in a strange place. At once his mind constructed from her manner, from her tone, from her temperament, the external surroundings of herself, her husband, and her daughter. He had a vision of a villa, dainty as a jewel-casket, with gaily-painted ceilings and cabinets of Sèvres china ; where everything had about it a bloom of newness, delicate as the youth in the bloom of a girl's complexion, and where the antiquity of the choicest artistic objects only gave them the charm of the rarest and the newest acquisitions. The difference was just this. To Carew, such objects in a drawing-room would suggest a dilapidated château ; to Mrs. Capel, such objects in a château suggested a possible drawing-room.

The General, as he talked to him, bore out this impression. It was quite evident that he was a man of taste and cultivation ; and he instantly named the painters of two small Dutch pictures which Carew, till that moment, had never looked at twice. He seemed well acquainted, too, with the history of the Revolution in France, and the position of the *noblesse* both before and after it. But the subject, though it commanded his interest, made no appeal to his sympathy. He treated it as calmly as if it were some geologic catastrophe: whilst as to the old towns, which he seemed so fond of visiting, it is true that he admired them for their picturesqueness and their curiosity; but in their associations he found nothing more personally touching to him than he would have probably found in some curious geologic formation.

Nor did Miss Capel in this way differ much from her parents, except that to her the strangeness and antiquity of the château seemed a source of imaginative and half-smiling alarm, which Carew, as he watched her, presently found himself admitting, became her almost as well as a feeling for its real meaning and history. And this impression grew on him. All the signs about him of a stately order of things which was well-nigh dead in France, and might soon be dying in England, possessed for himself so close and sad a significance, that there was, to his ears, a kind of fairy-like music in hearing them spoken of by a pair of lips so dainty merely as 'so odd' and 'so curious,' as if no sadness attached to them. He even smiled with pleasure as he caught in her soft eyes a floating flash of what seemed like unwilling amusement.

'I must,' she said, rising as soon as she had finished her tea, 'move about and examine everything for myself. Mr. Carew, you don't mind it—do you? I'll promise to be careful, and break absolutely nothing. Ah,' she exclaimed presently, 'what flowers! what roses! Mr. Carew, I like them best of all!'

Carew watched her as she stood close to the window, with her nostrils buried in a forest of crimson petals. She seemed like a creature fed on the breath of gardens. Then, turning round, with deliberate gliding waywardness, she moved here and there, inspecting one thing after another, till, at last, in the corner she caught sight of an old harpsichord. 'Will it play?' she asked, with a little cry of delight.

'Try,' said Carew. 'Let me open it for you.'

The instrument was certainly not in very good condition; but still Miss Capel contrived to elicit an air from it, that was not only distinctly an air, but an air full of plaintive pathos. Carew was much struck by this quick transition of sentiment, for her face as she looked at him seemed to take its expression from the music; and with some interest he asked what the air was. She did not stop playing, but, fixing her eyes on him with a

half-regretful mockery, ' Don't you know it?'
she said.   ' It is quite old, I believe.

> Si le Roi m'avoit donné
> Paris, sa grande ville—

The words come from Molière. Didn't he
live under the Monarchy—under the old *ré-gime*? I thought you were a Legitimist—isn't
that what you call it?—and that you cared for
all that sort of thing.   I wanted to prove to
you that I was not quite ignorant—not quite
unworthy of being a visitor at your château.'

Carew murmured that she had proved
that long ago. She had stopped playing now,
though her hands were still on the keys, and,
bending a little forward and looking at him
very gravely, ' Would you like me,' she said,
' to prove it to you still more conclusively?'

' You have proved it enough,' said Carew;
' but you can never prove it too often.   Yes,
please, prove it me in the way you say you
will.'

'I don't know,' she said, 'I don't know if I have the courage. I can't do it just at this moment at all events. I shall have to consult mamma.'

What she could mean he was utterly at a loss to conjecture; and she seemed to please herself in watching his baffled curiosity, which was only interrupted by the distant clang of the dressing-bell.

He had by this time recovered completely his yesterday's sense of her fascination. He now was convinced that she would distract without disturbing him, and he looked forward with interest to seeing her dressed for dinner. Her parents, however, both came down without her ; and Mrs. Capel with many apologies said she would be ready directly. But the minutes went by : no Miss Capel appeared ; and her mother at last insisted that dinner be kept waiting no longer for her. They had not, however, finished their soup when the defaulter entered ; and Carew could hardly repress an exclamation of delight and of astonishment. Anything so radiant, so bewildering, he had never seen in his life. She was powdered and patched, and her cheeks had a natural flush on them that was not rouge, and that made rouge unnecessary. Her dress was perfect, from the ribbon round her neck to the tips of her high-heeled shoes. She was a beauty of the Court of Louis Quinze come to life again ; and the way in which she bore herself made the spell complete. There was a little shyness in her entrance, but no awkwardness.   There was an expression in her eyes, in her movements even, half mischievous and half deprecating ; and she advanced to the table with all the grace of a child conscious of some misdemeanour and yet certain not to be punished for it.

' It's a dress,' said her mother, 'which she wore at a fancy ball at Paris. It is just like a picture in the gallery outside ; Violet noticed it the moment we came into the house, and nothing would satisfy her but to surprise you in it to-night.'

'I hope,' said Miss Capel, looking at Carew as she sat down, ' I hope you are not angry with me. I wanted to show you, as I told you at the piano, that I could make myself, at least superficially—is that the right word, I wonder ?—I dare say it isn't—that I could make myself superficially in keeping with an historic château.'

'Why,' said Carew by-and-by, 'can't we all go back to powder, and dress as they did a hundred years ago ? '

' We should have to change plenty of other things,' laughed the General, 'before we could manage that.'

' We should,' said Carew, 'and I should like plenty of other things changed.'

' How funny that would be ! ' said Miss

Capel, smiling at the idea. 'No—I don't want, myself, to go back to powder for always. It takes so long to do : you've no notion of what a time it takes. I don't think, indeed, that I want to go back at all, except—except——'

'Except what ?' said Carew, in a low tone of inquiry.

The General and his wife were at that moment speaking to each other, and Miss Capel, having cast a glance towards them, let her eyes rest on Carew's, and finished her broken sentence.

'We should all of us like, I suppose, to go back in our own lives for some things— to do them again, or not to do them at all.'

These words, and the manner in which she uttered them, remained in Carew's mind all through the course of dinner; and no sooner did the party find themselves in the drawing-room, than, pointing out to her a magnificent grand piano, 'I hope,' he said, 'you will go back far enough now, to play us that old song again. Perhaps, too, you would sing it to us.'

'I'm afraid,' she said, 'I have quite forgotten the words; but if you like, I will certainly sing you something—that is to say, if you don't make me feel too shy. What shall I sing?' she went on as Carew was opening the piano for her. 'Mamma, tell me what I shall sing.' And whilst she was speaking her fingers began touching the keys. Mrs. Capel was about to suggest a song, but before she could name it the musician had already begun one. It was quite different from anything Carew had expected, but in a second or two his senses confessed its witchery. It was in some Italian dialect, and moved to a tinkling air, as light and tender as the murmur of waves in moonlight. 'It is a little love-song,' she said, 'that is sung by Neapolitan fishermen. Do you like it? Here is another.' The other was of a different character, though apparently in the same dialect. To Carew the words meant nothing; but he could not mistake the sentiment, its plaintive melancholy, its mixture of rest and wistfulness; and the eyes of the singer, with a look of devotional abstraction in them, seemed to form unconsciously a part of the song themselves. But the object of the sentiment—as to that he was in doubt.

'What,' she said softly, when she had ended, 'do you think of that? Do you like it as well? It is an evening hymn the boatmen sing to the Virgin. It's the favourite song of my cousin, Madame de Saint Valery.'

'Tell me this,' he said by-and-by to her, as they were all preparing to retire. 'That hymn I like best of all your songs. Are you Catholics?'

'No, no,' she said, 'I don't know what we are. I don't suppose the General and mamma are anything. Can't one sing songs like that, and yet not be a Catholic?'

'But you,' he said, 'sang it with feeling—at least I thought so.'

'Do you ever,' she replied, 'read any of Shelley's poetry? If you do perhaps you have read these lines—

> The desire of the moth for the star,
> Of the night for the morrow ;
> A devotion to something afar
> From the sphere of our sorrow—

That is what, somehow, that song seems to mean to me.'

CHAPTER IV.

BY the following morning Carew was pretty clear in his mind as to where the charm lay that his new friends possessed for him; and he thought it over with a distinct if not a deep satisfaction, though the eyes of Miss Consuelo Burton were still watching him in the background. Their charm lay in the fact that whilst they sympathized with him on some points there were others, a whole set of them, in which they not only did not sympathize with him, but which it seemed they could not even comprehend. There was a total want in them of those social prejudices and attachments, and—it appeared—of those religious perplexities also, which were making all life in these latter days seem dark to him. They had no capital entrusted to those two disastrous vessels—a foundering aristocracy, and a religion that was already a derelict. The past to them was nothing more than a curiosity ; the changes of the present perplexed them with no personal problems: and Carew felt that in their company he caught their insensibility to his own sources of sorrow. He became conscious as he was dressing of a singular sense of emancipation. The sky of his mind grew suddenly blue and cloudless, and a world was breathing round him languid or bright with flowers. So vivid, indeed, was this last impression, that, with a fanciful wish to act literally in accordance with it, he had the actual flowers of the garden picked in increased profusion, in order to fill the rooms with scent and brilliant colour ; and the Capels had not been with him for four-and-twenty hours before a new spirit seemed to animate all the château.

His present disabled condition, though it proved to be nothing serious, prevented his making as yet any active efforts to entertain them; but, strange to say, no such efforts were needed. With the aid of his crutch he could move from room to room, and he was thus able to exhibit the contents of the house to them. Then the General had his own literary work to engage him ; and whenever his attention was not claimed elsewhere, he was perfectly happy in a little study that had been allotted to him. Both the ladies, too, with a tact that was half-thoughtfulness and half-instinct, did as their host begged them, and made themselves equally at home. Mrs. Capel brought down a gorgeous piece of embroidery, which she was copying from a Sicilian pattern ; and, seated near a window in an old gilt arm-chair, she was a perfect picture of contented and luxurious industry. As for Miss Capel, her ways, from Carew's point of view, though a little more restless, were not less satisfactory. She brought down a portfolio of music, which she turned over and discussed with him. Then again returning to her little hoard in her bedroom, she produced a pile of her favourite books of poetry ; and at last, having admitted that she drew, she was prevailed on to exhibit her sketches. Carew was surprised at the talent displayed in these —especially in some coloured portraits. ' If,' he said, ' you like to paint whilst you are here, there is an easel in one of the rooms, and a canvas stretched in readiness. The room itself would make a capital studio. You have just shown me your poets : it is there that I keep mine. Come and see it —will you? '

They went, and he found himself for the first time really alone with her. He was surprised at the pleasure the situation gave him. The room in question—the first of that suite of three which he had shown to his former guests as the scenes of his private labours, was hung with English chintz, and had old-fashioned English furniture. A century back it had been occupied by one of his great-great aunts. Miss Capel was delighted with it; but a farther door being open, she glided forwards and peeped into the room adjoining. 'More books!' she exclaimed, and she began to read the titles of them. These were Carew's treatises on philosophy and theology. She did not proceed far. With an odd incredulous smile she turned towards him and said, 'Do you really ever look into these? How funny of you! I can't imagine it.' Then with a little grimace of mock determination and wilfulness, 'Now,' she said, 'I am going to open this other door. This is your Bluebeard's room, perhaps, where you keep your beheaded wives.' She opened the door, but closed it almost instantly. 'Oh,' she said, 'that's nothing. That's just like a lawyer's office. I suppose it's the place where you add all your accounts up. No, no—here is the room I like,' and she went back again to the one they had first entered. 'Do you know, 'she exclaimed, 'this looks exactly like a home —not, I mean, a home that I have ever had myself; but like what I imagine an English home must be. Oh ! and, Mr. Carew, you have got my dear Shelley here !'

'You shall make this your home,' said Carew, 'as long as you stay with me. It shall be your own room.'

'Do you think,' she replied, 'one can make a home in three days ?'

'Three days !' he said. 'You must stay

longer than that. Now I have you here I am not going to let you go. See, there is the easel, in case you should care to use it.'

She gave a slight start, as if a new thought had occurred to her. Then she looked at him for a few moments in silence, with all the while an ambushed laugh in her eyes. At last she said:

'If you will sit to me, I will try and make a picture of you. Not now—I don't mean that—but to-morrow. You mustn't mind, though, if it's a very bad one—all out of drawing—one shoulder higher than the other. I'm not able to flatter.'

'You mean not with your pencil?'

'I don't think,' she said gravely, still keeping her eyes on him, 'that I could flatter *you* in any way. How could I? What could you care for anything I said to you?'

She stopped short abruptly, and her gaze wandered away from him, something as that of a kitten does when its eye is caught by a butterfly. 'Oh !' she said, 'how delicious ! Is not that a guitar in the corner ? I used to play the guitar. Let me take it to mamma and show it to her.'

'Presently,' said Carew.

'No,' she said, smiling, 'not presently, but now—instantly, Mr. Carew—instantly.'

He could hardly believe his senses. She moved quietly up to him and gently touched his arm to emphasize her wish that he should be moving. But what struck him far more than the familiarity of the action was the total want in it of any suggestion of bold-ness. It suggested nothing but an almost unconscious trust, and the moment the first shock of surprise was over he felt as he would have felt had he been touched by some soft wild animal. He was sorry that the *tête-à-tête* should be ended ; but there was a sort of plea-sure even in obeying her command to end it.

Chemists tell us that at a touch a liquid will sometimes crystallize. A touch will produce sometimes as great a change in feelings. Everything the girl did, however slight and trivial—her words, her smiles, her gestures, the smallest occupation she shared with him, even her playing Beggar-my-neighbour, as she did with him that evening—all became full of some magical and indefinable charm. She was not only freeing his spirit from its natural load of cares, but she was gradually lulling and refreshing it with some undreamt-of melody. What the melody meant he was in no hurry to ask himself. In its uncertainty lay some part of its spell. He only knew, when, on this second night of her visit, he looked back on the day which had just been ended, that although on the surface there were none but the most trivial incidents, yet its memory was to him a mosaic of coloured moments.

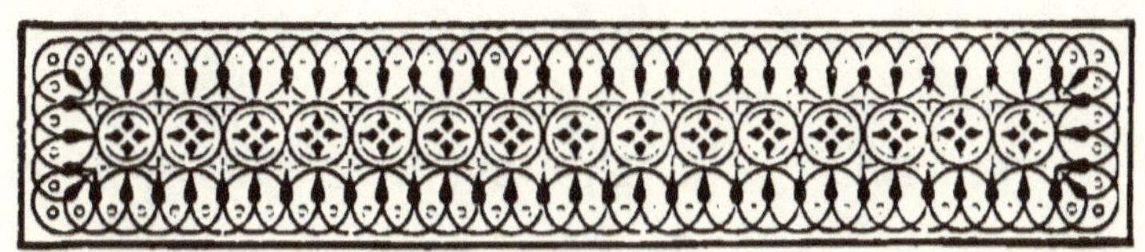

CHAPTER V.

THE day which followed was superficially just as tranquil; but under the surface he found it even more bewildering. It was iridescent with new sensations. The General talked pleasantly at meals, and talked pleasantly over his cigarette afterwards. In the intervals of sociability he retired to his notes and papers; his wife sat in the gilt arm-chair at her embroidery, diffusing around her an atmosphere of suave and refined contentment; once or twice there was a little music; coffee was drunk on the ramparts in the bright afternoon sunshine; in the evening the guitar was strung and played upon; and finally there was a rubber of whist. Meanwhile, during the course of the morning, Carew's portrait had been begun, in the chintz-hung studio.

So far as events went, this was the whole day's chronicle; and if the conversation which went with them had come to be written down, it would, for the most part, have seemed equally insignificant. This was the case with what passed in private between the sitter and the artist, just as much as with what passed when they were all together. Indeed, to Carew one of Miss Capel's chief attractions was that with her, conversation came so naturally that it left behind it no lasting trace in his memory—nothing but a wake of laughing and disappearing ripples. It was less an intentional interchange of thoughts than a natural result of the contact of two lives. It was little more conscious than the sound of meeting waters, or than the blush that comes on the cheek of health or pleasure.

But though its details, for the most part, made but little impression upon him, yet, taken as a whole, a very strong impression indeed was produced by, or at least produced along with, it. Carew felt that her character was becoming gradually clear to him, like a summer landscape appearing through a gauzy mist. He was conscious of an odd mixture in her of gaiety and of wondering tenderness. She seemed constantly to be struck with the humorous side of a world of which personally she had had no rude experience ; and her fancy moved with a kind of mischievous buoyancy, like a star of sunlight dipping and floating upon the sea. Indeed, she somehow conveyed the idea that all life had been a playground to her, into which she had been turned loose ; and that what she divined or knew of its sadness and its deeper realities she had found out for herself in the course of a lonely holiday.

It was not by her words only that this impression was conveyed. It was conveyed by her looks, and the naïve grace of her movements—sometimes by their infantine petulance, and by the childish mishaps which, as she bent over her drawing, would bring her light cloud of hair straying downwards across her eyes.

There was something more also. Here and there in the middle of her ordinary conversation—her musical succession of unremembered sentences—a sentence would escape her of quite a different kind, which shone out from among the others like a coloured lamp amongst leaves, and made them flush with the hue of its own suggestions. These sentences stamped themselves on Carew's mind ; and tended to make the girl's character a puzzle to him. What, for instance, he asked, could she have been thinking of when, at dinner, she said that most people would be glad to go back in their lives for some things—to do them again, or not to do them at all? And now, when she was drawing him, she once looked solemnly up at him, and said without a smile or any symptom of flinching:

'Mr. Carew, I want you to tell me something. Do you think I am very forward?'

'Forward!' he said, laughing. 'No. Why should I think you so?'

'I think it was very forward of me to say I would do your picture. I should have waited, if I had wished to do it—and I did wish that; I wished it very much—and I should have fished for you to ask me.'

'Why,' he asked, 'do you think you should have done that?'

'Other people would have done so,' she said, 'wouldn't they? You must know.

Other people wouldn't tell a man that they wanted to do his picture. Mamma would say that it wasn't modest to do so—or proper —I think that's her word. Mamma thinks at times that I'm not at all a proper person. Proper!' she repeated, as if thinking the matter over—'I can't tell what's proper. I always say out just what I think.'

'And so,' Carew persisted, 'you did wish to draw me, then?'

'I did,' she said, quite simply. 'I wished to draw you the moment you mentioned drawing. Yes,' she added, 'from quite the very first moment. Mr. Carew, sit still. I am trying to get your mouth.'

What, thought Carew, did this little episode betoken? Had she been a coquette of the most accomplished kind, she could hardly have introduced in a more decided way that element into their acquaintance which a coquette would desire to find in it.

A similar incident happened late in the afternoon. Carew had retired to his room to write a number of business letters; the General and his wife had been occupied in the same way; and Miss Capel had gone off for a short walk by herself, to do a little exploration on her own account. She returned at about five o'clock, and found the others round the tea-table. She had on her hat and gloves, and she paused in the doorway, leaning on a slim gold-headed walking-stick.

'May I come in?' she said, 'or must I go up and change my things?'

'Come in,' said Carew, 'come in.'

But she still stood there for a moment, as if she were bent on tantalizing him.

'I'm longing,' she said, 'to tell Mr. Carew all the places I've been to. I'm positively longing.'

'Well,' said Carew, 'don't keep us all

in the draught. Suppose that you shut the door and give us a description of your wanderings.'

She began to do this as well as she could, and up to a certain point he saw clearly the path she had taken ; but when she had brought herself to the edge of a neighbouring wood, when she followed the windings of a certain shadowy footpath, and at last arrived at an old ruinous fountain, he could only conceive that her description was faulty, or admit that she had hit on a spot which was as yet unknown to himself.

' Mamma,' she exclaimed at last, ' what do you think ? I know the grounds of Mr. Carew's castle better than he knows them himself. If,' she continued, speaking to him only, ' you are able to walk before I go away, I will take you to my fountain, and show you I have not invented it.   Will you come ? '

Carew said ' Yes.'

'I don't believe you will,' she replied. 'Men never mean what they say. But I should like to take you. Yes, I am determined to take you. Fancy,' she added, as if the reflection pleased her, 'fancy my taking Mr. Carew for a walk!'

She had asked him already if he considered her forward, and her present proposal recalled the question to his mind. He smiled as, looking into her clear eyes, he thought of it. He would as soon have attributed forwardness to a blue-eyed child in its cradle.

The walk at once assumed a prominent place in his prospects. He thought how delightful it would be to be lost in some lonely wood with her. His ankle, however, still kept him a cripple, so though he would willingly have gone off at once with her, he had to postpone the pleasure at any rate till to-morrow. The rest of the day passed much

like the earlier part of it, except that, in a way
he was hardly conscious of, his intimacy with
his companion was growing silently closer,
and every idle and unregarded hour added a
thread to the chain that was fast binding
them.   He would have accepted the situation
for the present, enjoying without examining
it ; but, during the evening, once again she
startled him.

She had been singing a little, and he was
standing by her at the piano.   A song had
been just ended ; he was engaged in looking
out another for her, and she was striking a
few careless chords in the interval.   Presently
some instinct made him turn and look at her.
She was watching him intently, and he felt
that she had been doing so for some moments.
When their eyes met she showed no sign of
confusion.   She only smiled a little, but she
did not withdraw her gaze.   It remained as
steadfast as if Greuze had painted it.   At

last she began softly humming to the stray notes as she struck them, and then, abruptly, but in a tone equally soft :

' I am not,' she said, ' going to do any more to your picture.'

' Why not ? ' he asked.

After a pause she answered him.

' Because,' she said, making a louder noise with the chords, 'because—do you know this, Mr. Carew ?—it's very bad for me to look at you. I am not going to do so—ever—ever—ever any more.'

' Never any more ! ' said Carew.

' Of course,' she said, laughing, ' I shall look at you enough to avoid running against you in the passage, or spilling any slops over you when I come for more tea. I shall look at you just enough, perhaps, to prevent your thinking me rude. But that's all. Do you understand ? '

' No,' said Carew, ' I don't, and I don't

believe it. Why do you say that it is bad for you to look at me?'

'For many reasons,' she said, 'for many, many reasons.' She stopped playing suddenly, and he heard a faint sigh come from her. 'You couldn't understand them. Men can understand nothing. No, Mr. Carew, no picture to-morrow.'

'Come,' said the voice of Mrs. Capel from the farther end of the room, 'we are waiting for another song, Violet. Are you not going to give us one?'

'No,' said Miss Capel, rising, 'I have no more voice, mamma. I have sung enough for this evening. Have you the key of my album? I am going to show Mr. Carew my photographs.'

'It is upstairs,' said her mother, 'on my chain, where you asked me to put it. If you want to show your photographs, you must do so to-morrow.'

'Very well, then,' she said, 'I will show him my poetry books over again. I don't believe he has half looked at them.'

'No,' said Carew, 'I am sure I have not seen this one.'

She tried to take it from him, but he was too quick for her. 'Why,' he asked, 'don't you want me to look at it?'

'Oh,' she said, 'it is not what you would care for.' He read the title. It was 'Songs of the Soul's Life.'

'Look at it if you like,' she went on. 'Oh, there are no secrets in it.' He found it was a selection from various well-known writers, of poems bearing on moral and spiritual struggles; and he noted, with some wonder, as he turned the pages over, that they were marked in many places. 'Are they your marks?' he asked.

'Some,' she said, gently but indifferently.

'Most, I think, were made by the person who gave the book to me.'

'I like this,' said Carew—'this poem on Prayer;' and he paused, reading a sonnet which had first arrested his eye by the deep lines underscoring its last couplet. The couplet itself, when he read it, he found even more striking. It was this:

> Is there a wish for which you dare not pray?
> Then pray to God to take that wish away.

He raised his eyes to Miss Capel, in half-incredulous wonder as to what such a passage could possibly have to do with her. She seemed to understand the look, and said with a trace of flippancy, 'I don't know what it was I was supposed to wish for, so dreadful that I might not pray for it.'

'Mr. Carew,' Mrs. Capel here interposed, 'do you know what the time is? It is actually past eleven. You must allow me to say good-night to you. I must take off Violet too;

and you must finish your discussions, and she must show you her photographs, to-morrow.'

'I had thought,' said Carew, ' that to-morrow we might manage a little picnic to a place on the sea just beyond Nice, called Beaulieu. There will be time, however, to settle about that in the morning. Look, Miss Capel : since I am not to inspect your album, I shall take upstairs with me a certain volume of poetry.'

Before he went to sleep he turned to the same sonnet, again wondering what could be its application to her. Then he glanced at some of the other poems ; but his whole attention was suddenly drawn away from them by an inscription on the fly-leaf, and a copy of verses under it, plainly in a man's handwriting. The verses were dated Calais, the Christmas Day of two years ago, and the inscription was simply, ' To V. C. at Naples.' The verses were not remarkable

for much literary excellence, but they kept
Carew wakeful for many hours that night.
They were as follows :

> *Yesterday a cloudless sky was glowing,*
>   *All the flowers were flowering yesterday;*
> *And to-day a bitter east is blowing,*
>   *Flowerless all the flowers, the skies are grey.*
> *Yesterday there breathed a life beside me —*
>   *Now the lips and eyes are far away.*
> *Deep in memories of the past I hide me,*
> *And I pray for her, whate'er betide me,*
>   *Every wish for which I dare to pray.*

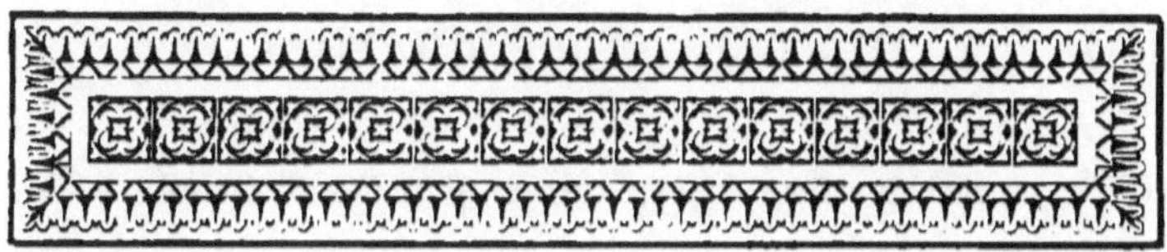

CHAPTER VI.

IF Carew was inclined, and indeed he was inclined, to allow the verses to haunt him the following morning, the arrival of the post at once put them out of his mind, and for the time being gave him something more pressing to think about. The General, it appeared, had received a letter from Genoa, which begged him to come there some days sooner than he had intended. Having followed him from Nice to Cannes, and from Cannes on to the château, it had been considerably delayed upon the road; and if he were to act on the urgent request contained in it, he and his party would have to start immediately.

Here was, indeed, a blow to Carew's whole prospects. The enchanting cup that was being just raised to his lips was to be dashed at once to the ground, before he had more than tasted the foam of it. He anxiously asked the General if the matter was very pressing. It was, the General said ; it was a matter not of pleasure, but of business. He was largely interested in the Genoese Tramways, and there was to be a meeting of the shareholders, at which he must be present if possible. The meeting had been at first fixed for Friday; the date had now been altered to Tuesday ; to-day was Sunday ; and, accordingly, at the latest, it would be absolutely necessary for them to leave by to-morrow evening.

As soon as Carew learnt that it was a matter of business, a ray of hope again brightened the situation. Why, he asked, should the General not go alone, leave his wife and daughter at the château behind him, and return to them, and finish his visit, on his way back to Cannes? Why not? There was only one valid answer, and that was their fear of trespassing on their host's hospitality. This was expressed in the most courteous and delicate way, and Carew could see that it was perfectly unaffected. The same was apparent, however, with regard to his own wishes; and as soon as the General and his wife were convinced that such was the case, they agreed to his plan with almost as much pleasure as he himself evinced when he saw that they were going to do so.

'And now,' he went on, 'that being settled satisfactorily, what do you say to this as a little scheme for to-morrow? I was talking last night about a picnic at Beaulieu. Now the General's train, which leaves Nice about five, passes Beaulieu about twenty minutes later.   What I propose is that we go there for our picnic to-morrow, and leave the General, on our way home, at the station.'

This, again, seemed perfectly satisfactory, and nothing was wanting but to communicate the arrangements to Miss Capel.   She, however, was not to be seen.   She had left the room, without saying a word, the moment she had heard the contents of her father's letter, and it was presently found, on inquiring, that she had gone out of doors.

'You are beginning, Mr. Carew,' said Mrs. Capel, 'to walk so much better again. Why don't you go out and look for her? She's sure to be on the terrace.   Poor child, she will be in raptures with all your kindness! The General and I shall have some letter-writing to get over.   Do, Mr. Carew, go out and look for Violet.'

'I suppose,' smiled the General as he was

preparing to go off with his wife, 'this being Sunday, we ought to be all at church. But my motto has always been that of the monks, *Qui laborat orat.* It is about the only piece of monkery that applies to the modern world.'

Carew was no sooner left alone than he went out eagerly, and began a search for Miss Capel. He walked several times round the château ; he asked the men at the stables if she had gone down the front drive, and he then descended into the mazy walks of the gardens ; but he could neither see nor hear of her. Meanwhile his thoughts went straying back to that day a week ago, and to the scene at morning Mass ; and all life, with its changes, began to seem to him like a dream, so quickly did one phantom supplant another in it, so readily did the phantom he was even now seeking elude him.

At last, out of spirits, he again mounted to the ramparts, hoping, but hoping in vain,

for Miss Capel's figure somewhere. There
was not a soul stirring. He was standing on
the spot from which, such a short while since,
his grand party had watched the display of
fireworks. Just under the walls were the
tiled roofs of the village, and a bare patch of
ground, where the children were accustomed
to play. It chanced that here he looked over
the parapet, and down below, seated on a
broken mill-stone, he saw Miss Capel talking to a little sun-browned child. He was
about to call her, but his voice checked
itself. For a moment he remained watching her. Her bright spotted dress and her
parasol lying beside her gave a charm to
the sight merely as a piece of colour ; but
what specially struck him was a sad tenderness in her attitude, and still more in the
smile that he saw was playing upon her face,
like the upward flickering light reflected from
running water. At last he uttered her name.

She looked up and rose; and patting the child on the cheek, pointed to a neighbouring turret, through which, by a narrow stair, there was a way up to the ramparts. Carew went forward to meet her. Her movements were more quick than his, and when he reached the top of the stair she was just emerging. Her face was sadder than he had ever seen it before. Her eyes shone with a light that suggested recent tears, and her cheeks were like flowers that had just been rained upon.

'I have been looking for you,' he said, 'everywhere. Where on earth have you been?'

She turned her head towards the village. 'I have been to church,' she said.

'Alone? And why did you not let us know that you were going?'

'What would have been the good?' she said. '*They* never go, and I don't suppose you do. I do everything alone.'

Carew looked at her with a new sensation of wonder. 'You have not been alone,' he said gently, 'since you have been here, have you?'

'That,' she murmured, 'will be all over to-morrow.'

'No, it won't,' he exclaimed with a sudden glow of delight as he discerned the extent of the regret he was about to dispel. 'I have been trying to find you everywhere on purpose to tell you this. You and your mother are to stay here with me. Your father is to go to Genoa by himself; after that he is going to come back here ; and as for to-morrow, we are all of us going for a picnic, and shall set him down at Beaulieu station in the evening.'

She looked at first as if she could hardly believe the news. But presently the sun once more shone out in her eyes; her whole face made an artless confession of pleasure ; and gently coming close to him, she so extended her hand that he for a short moment took it in both of his.

'Tell me,' he said to her by-and-by when luncheon was ended, 'are you going to do any more to my picture, or are you not ?'

'You can walk now,' she said, 'so I am going to take you out walking—that is to say, if you will come. I am going to show you the fountain I discovered, and which you believe I have invented. No,' she went on, in answer to his glance towards her parents, 'they are not coming. They have papers—business— all sorts of things to settle this afternoon. You must come with me quite by yourself; unless you think you will be too much bored with my company. Mamma, do you hear this ? I am going to show Mr. Carew his own fountain.'

When she first began to speak, there had seemed something half clandestine in her pro- posal ; but, though she was evidently pleased at the prospect of being alone with him, the idea of concealment had apparently not entered her mind.

'Go, then,' said Mrs. Capel, 'and put your things on quickly : or else you will be losing the best part of the day. You always take so long in getting yourself ready for anything. Come, Mr. Carew, whilst Violet is upstairs you shall see that book of her photographs which she wanted to exhibit to you last night.'

Carew with considerable interest watched the unlocking of the volume. His quick eye, amongst the opening pages, at once caught a vision of landscapes, yachts, and faces, and of these last, he hardly knew how or why, he received an impression that the greater number were men. 'That,' said Mrs. Capel, beginning at the very beginning, 'that is the General's yacht. The picture was done at Naples. You see Violet there, in a sailor's hat, under the awning. That group—I dare say you can see where that was done—it was in the Club garden at Cowes. Violet is there too—a little in the background. There are some other faces there which I dare say you will recognize.'

Mrs. Capel was right; he did recognize some of them; and they were not faces that it gave him much pleasure to see. Then followed views of various continental towns, such as Trouville, Homburg, and Florence; and the views of each town were accompanied by some groups, as a souvenir; several of which had been taken, it seemed, at races, and in all of which Miss Capel's figure was visible. To these succeeded some pages of single portraits. They were mostly men, as Carew had imagined they would be. They were also mostly foreigners; and he fancied that he could catch a trace of pique in his voice as, passing from one languishing young exquisite to another, he asked, ' Who is this ? ' or ' Pray, and who may that be ?'   Mrs. Capel spoke of none of them with much enthusiasm ; and was passing them rapidly over, in search for a château in Hungary, in which, she said, they had passed the previous autumn, when Carew exclaimed, 'Wait just for one moment.   Who was that man—the one you turned over this instant ?'

'Which?' said Mrs. Capel.

'Not a young man—an old man—a man with a black moustache, and exceedingly well-curled hair.   This one—yes, this is the one I mean.'

'What,' said Mrs. Capel, with a tone of slight embarrassment, 'do you find to interest you there ?   Do you think it's a wise face ?'

'Surely,' said Carew, 'that must be the Prince de Vaucluse, the grandson of Napoleon's old army-contractor.   I thought I saw him in that group in the club garden at Cowes.'

' You are right,' Mrs. Capel began, but she was interrupted by a voice over her shoulder. ' Mamma,' it said, ' what are you showing my book to Mr. Carew for ?—and that page too ? Please shut it up. Why need you be always turning to it ? And the key— I must have my key. Remember, mamma,' she said, with a smile as she took it, ' I am never going to let that out of my own possession again. And now—now, if Mr. Carew's quite ready, I'm going to take him off for this walk I told him of.'

Carew had rarely enjoyed a moment more than that when they found themselves together in the open air, his companion's eyes glancing close beside him, and the scented pine-wood, for whose shade they were bound, fronting them. Miss Capel, he found, had been quite correct in her description. She had made what to him was quite a new dis- covery, and at the end of a path which had possibly once been gravelled, but which now was nothing more than a neglected clearing in the underwood, an abrupt turn brought them to a little hollow or dingle, its entrance guarded by two mutilated statues. There, embedded in a bank of rocks and ferns, was the fountain of which Miss Capel had spoken. It was an old basin, gleaming with dark water, and arched over by a shell-shaped canopy of brickwork.

'Look, Mr. Carew,' she exclaimed, 'don't you call this delicious? Don't you thank me very much for having discovered it?'

'I thank you,' he said, looking at her with a gravity he was hardly conscious of, 'I thank you far more for having come yourself to show it me.'

The words seemed to sink into her like a stone into deep water, and she returned his look with a sort of wondering gratitude.

'Mr. Carew,' she murmured at last, 'how

can you say such things ? It is you who ought to be thanked for coming to walk with me.'

She had seated herself on the rim of the basin, and now, looking down into the dark and gloomy reflections, she began to splash the water with the tip of her parasol. At last Miss Capel, not raising her eyes, but still watching the water and continuing to play with it, said with a forced flippancy, 'Well, Mr. Carew, will you have the kindness to make a remark?'

'I was,' he said, 'just going to do so. I was looking last night at that collection of poems you have. You know the book I mean, don't you?' She assented. 'I was reading,' he went on, 'the verses at the beginning —those in manuscript. I see you have an accomplished poet amongst your friends.'

'The person who wrote that,' she said gently, 'was no friend of mine : and I should have torn those verses out if they hadn't been rather pretty. It's horribly ungrateful of me to say so; for he wished to do me good. He wished to improve me. He thought me, I believe, very wicked. But one can't be grateful merely because one ought to be. Can one, Mr. Carew?'

'May I ask,' he said, 'who the person was?'

'Certainly,' she replied carelessly, 'there's not the least secret about it.'

'Then was it the Prince de Vaucluse?'

'The Prince!' she exclaimed, with a light ironical laugh. 'What a notion! I don't suppose he knows what poetry is—except that it's something which has nothing to do with races. Besides, the Prince thinks me so perfect that there is no need to improve me. No— the person who wrote those verses was a sort of cousin of the General's—an English cousin.'

'Oh!' said Carew, relieved, 'a relation of yours.'

'Didn't you know?' she said, 'and yet I suppose you didn't—how should you?—that the General is not my father? He is only my step-father. I took his name, and he is going to leave some money to me. There's another interesting fact which, perhaps, you did not know either. I'm an heiress. Mr. Carew, I'm afraid you're not attending. Why are you knocking those leaves about with your stick? Don't you find all this that I tell you very exciting?'

'No,' said Carew, with a certain dryness in his tone, 'I can't say I do.'

'Mr. Carew,' she said. He looked up at her, and he saw in her eyes a soft provoking mockery. 'Are you,' she went on, 'not a fortune-hunter?'

'Should you wish,' he said, 'to be married for the sake of your fortune?'

'I think,' she murmured, her voice getting tender again for an instant, 'I think it would be too horrible. However, don't pity me. There is no chance of that ever happening.'

'How do you know that?' he said.

'How do I know that!' she repeated deliberately, and in a manner that was half absent and half teasing. 'Perhaps I don't know it; perhaps I only conjecture. Or, Mr. Carew, this is just possible—perhaps I know it because I am already bespoken. *Bespoke—bespoken*—which is the right thing to say?'

Carew was seated on the trunk of a fallen tree, his eyes fixed on the ground. He neither looked up nor spoke. He merely continued the application of his stick to the leaves with an air of deeper preoccupation.

'Mr. Carew,' said Miss Capel, after some moments' silence, 'why don't you answer my question?'

'What question? I was not aware that you had asked me any.'

'Yes, I did. I asked you a question of grammar. Which is it right to say—*bespoke* or *bespoken*?'

Carew muttered something that was like the shadow of an oath, and struck his stick on the ground with such violence as to break it. When next Miss Capel spoke the tone of her voice was changed. It was soft, regretful, tender.

'Are you angry?' she said. 'Why should you be?'

'I am not angry,' said Carew, in a constrained voice, rising and turning away from her.

'Yes, you are,' she said; and she slipped down from her seat, and, going up to him, looked him full in the face. 'You are angry. Will you please not be?' She put out her hand, and held him by one of the buttons of his coat. 'Mr. Carew, will you please not to be angry any longer ? I want you, if you will, to let me do one thing.'

'Well,' he said, taking her hand and smiling.

'I want you to allow me to go on doing your picture. Come in, will you? Do you mind? If only the light lasts, I might do a little now.'

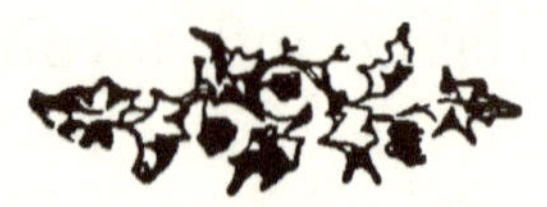

CHAPTER VII.

THEY were to start for the picnic by eleven o'clock next day, and the carriage, freighted with hampers, was waiting at the door punctually.

'The General and Violet will be down directly,' said Mrs. Capel to Carew as she entered the drawing-room. 'Will you kindly fasten this last hook of my cloak for me? Thank you.'

Then, as if the performance of the slight office had put him for the moment on a footing of greater intimacy with her, she laid her hand on her daughter's locked book of photographs, and said rather sadly :

'You know the Prince de Vaucluse, do you?'

'Hardly,' said Carew. 'But he was once to be seen about a good deal in London society.'

'Of course,' said Mrs. Capel, 'of course I know all that, and he is now one of the very smartest men in Paris.'

'My acquaintance with him,' said Carew, 'was confined to seeing him at "The Travellers," where every afternoon he filled up a large arm-chair—I see him now with the light on his turquoise rings—and drank sweet curaçoa out of a claret-glass.'

'I hope,' said Mrs. Capel, 'that he's better in that way now. He's a great admirer of Violet's. In fact, he is engaged to be married to her.'

'Indeed!' said Carew, trying to speak with indifference. 'When?'

Mrs. Capel raised her eyebrows with an odd expression of gentle but unwilling resignation.

'Not yet,' she said, 'not yet. The General insisted that she should wait for some months longer. If the Prince likes, he will be allowed to claim her in May ; but I hope myself—well, we shall see what happens. I can't imagine, for my own part, what my child can see in him.'

She had hardly finished speaking when the General and Miss Capel appeared, and in a few moments they had all set off on their expedition. The day was so bright and exhilarating, and the country looked so beautiful, that expressions of admiration and pleasure supplied at first the equivalent to an animated conversation ; but after this came the usual succession of silences, and then Carew began to turn his thoughts inwards, and ask himself what effect Mrs. Capel's news had had on him. He had not been quite unprepared for it ; but, all the same, when he heard it it affected him something like a slight electric shock. He was, however, further aware of this : the shock, being slight, had not been wholly disagreeable. It contained, no doubt, elements of pain, of pique, of disappointment, and of jealousy ; but through all these there came tingling a sensation of triumph and of possession. That lovely form that was breathing and blushing close to him, those eyes with the colour and light in them of a tremulous morning sea—he was sure, or he was almost sure, that, whoever might claim them some day, for the present moment they belonged to him more completely than to anybody else in the world ; and every smile, movement, or rippling laugh of hers seemed like a music that was part of his own life.

This feeling, through the whole course of the drive—this feeling of his possession of *her*—was constantly receiving food from the countless minute ways in which she seemed to assume possession of *him*. Most of them were wholly imperceptible to anyone but their two selves. Sometimes, however, they were more open and undisguised, and Carew was surprised, on more than one occasion, at her almost parading—so it seemed—the footing on which she was with him.

'Mr. Carew, talk,' she said, after he had been silent for longer than usual. ' Say something to amuse us ; or, if you can't do that, to instruct us. You won't ? Well, repeat us a piece of poetry.'

'Violet,' exclaimed Mrs. Capel, ' Mr. Carew will think you a lunatic.'

'Mamma,' Miss Capel continued, apparently not hearing the interruption, 'if Mr. Carew won't repeat any poetry, I will repeat some. Listen !'

And with a grave face and a demure mechanical sing-song, she began :

> ' Yesterday a cloudless sky was glowing,
>   All the flowers were flowering yesterday ;
> And to-day a bitter east is blowing—

Blowing—blowing—blowing. Mamma—Mr. Carew—don't you think that's beautiful ? I call it most touching. I don't know what you do.'

A slight shade of annoyance passed over Carew's face, and Mrs. Capel again interposed with a remonstrance. But the girl's eyes were full of a mischievous determination, and, with a graceful doggedness, she repeated the aimless question. 'Don't you think those verses are very touching ? See, I try to make conversation, and no one will keep it up. Mr. Carew, if you don't like poetry, suppose we try grammar. Tell us something, will you, about the auxiliary verbs ?'

'Violet !' exclaimed Mrs. Capel, actually frowning, for a wonder, 'we shall think you are gone crazy.'

'Mr. Carew, mamma, is a great authority on English grammar, and he gave me a lecture yesterday—or, rather, he would not give me a lecture—on the formation of the past participle.'

When this conversation was taking place they were fast nearing their destination, and Carew was here obliged to stand up, in order to give the coachman some directions about the road. The scene of the picnic was to be a certain secluded spot, almost hidden by woods, at the end of a long promontory. It was hard to find, to anyone who did not know the locality, and his guidance was now required almost constantly till they arrived at it. The subject of English grammar was, therefore, allowed to drop; but just as the carriage drew up, and the door was being forced open, Miss Capel said, with the same look in her eyes, 'Mr. Carew, I want you to tell us this. Which is right—*bespoke* or *bespoken* ?'

The look, the tone, the question, all jarred upon Carew. He could not tell why, but, each and all, they irritated him, and half the charm of the drive seemed tarnished by this incident at its ending. To hide such a feeling he set himself with double diligence to help the servants in unpacking the hampers ; but when Miss Capel came to join in the operation, he could not, try as he would, keep a slight frost from his manner.

She, for her part, seemed not to notice this, and all her former appealing ways had returned to her, though he might have detected in them a certain trace of timidity. He did detect it at last, but not till after many minutes of blindness. He detected it in her gentle, almost humble tone, when she asked him if he would help her in carrying some bottles of wine, which it was thought advisable to cool in a brook close by. He did as she asked him, and they walked off together, and arranged their bottles in a satisfactory position ; then, just as they were about to go back again, she laid her hand on his arm, and, looking into his eyes sadly, ' Are you angry,' she said, ' because I teased you in the carriage? Nobody but you knew what I was laughing at. It's not that I want to laugh ; I can tell you that truly. Mr. Carew, please not to be angry with me any more.'

The effect of the prayer was instant, and when they returned to the table-cloth, which was by this time well covered with dishes, the cloud that had gathered between them had quite melted away. The General and Mrs. Capel were both charmed with the spot, and were full of Carew's praises for his happy judgment in choosing it. It was a little grassy common jutting into the sea, like a mulberry-leaf. It was tufted with gorse and rosemary, and backed by a belt of fir-woods ; and the woods, with their faint smell of turpentine and their murmur, mixed in the morning air with the smell and murmur of the sea.

The luncheon passed off in the most agreeable manner possible, and the General, when it was over, brought out his cigar-case. His eye had been caught by a distant mountain fort which was being constructed on one of the heights above Nice; and the taste of tobacco having unloosed his tongue, he was soon giving Carew an elaborate lecture on the various errors the engineers had committed. Carew's civility was put to a severe test. He had promised himself a walk all alone with Miss Capel, and now what had happened? He could hardly even steal a look at her. At last matters came to a crisis. She rose, opened her parasol, and strolled away by herself. But the General still went on; he was on a favourite subject; and, to crown all, he presently made Carew walk off with him, and away from Miss Capel, to a distance, in order to get a glimpse of the harbour works at Villefranche. Carew felt as he went that his feet were made of lead. He could hardly force them to go on this most unwilling pilgrimage, and never before had ten minutes seemed so much like two long hours to him. At last, however, he was back again at the scene of the luncheon. Mrs. Capel was still sitting there, attentively reading a copy of the 'Baltimore Weekly Sun'; but as for Miss Capel, what had become of her? This was the question which Carew asked at once. Mrs. Capel looked slowly round.

'I don't know,' she said; ' she has gone off somewhere by herself.'

'Ah!' said Carew, ' there she is, just going round that point.'

'I believe,' said Mrs. Capel, ' there's an old tower she wants to look at. Go to her, Mr. Carew; go and help her. The General and I will follow you. I walk rather slowly; and besides, I want to show him an article in this paper.'

Carew did not wait to be told twice. He

was off at a rapid pace in the direction of
the disappearing figure, which, clearly defined
with its outlines against the sea, had all the
distinctness of an object quite near, and yet
impressed the imagination as if it were very
far off.   It was some moments before she
caught sight of him, but when she did so
she at once stood still.   When he came up to
her, her face was bright with a smile, and her
very soul seemed in her eyes, greeting him :
but at the same time she was panting, and
pressing her hand to her heart.

'I thought,' she said, ' you were not going
to come at all.'

' It was the General kept me,' said Carew.
' Are you out of breath ?'

' No,' she said, ' it is only that I was so
glad when I saw you coming at last. Do
I look glad ? I'm afraid I do—a great deal
too glad. I can never hide my feelings—
never ; that's the worst of me.'

'I wish,' said Carew, 'I could but believe that.'

'What ?—that that is the worst of me ? '

'No,' he said, 'but that you really show your feelings—perhaps I should say, that you really feel what you show.'

'I have not,' she said, ' hidden them from you, certainly. I have shown them a great deal too plainly.'

' To-day, for instance,' said Carew, 'in the carriage.'

' What, Mr. Carew : are you angry about that still—because I teased you about those verses ? Why should you be ? I could tease you again now. It was not that I wanted to laugh, as I said before to you. I was much more inclined to cry. But men are so dense, they never understand anything.'

They were making their way up a rugged and rocky slope, on the brow of which stood the tower which Miss Capel desired to reach ;

and the difficulties of the scramble made a pause here in the conversation. The first to speak again was Carew, and he did so just as they were at the dark door of the building.

' I understand one thing,' he said, ' I do understand one thing.'

' What thing ?' she asked.

' I understand,' he said—' we have not decided how to put it grammatically—I understand that you *are* bespoken.'

Her cheeks flushed, and her sensitive lips parted, not to speak, but merely in helpless trouble. At the same moment she was spared from attempting any answer to him by a quavering voice which was heard addressing them from the interior; and directly afterwards an old woman appeared, who lived in the tower, and was accustomed to show it to visitors. They followed her in, and she began her usual explanations—how the tower was built in the reign of Louis the Fourteenth; how there was once a fort round it, and so on; and how the Great Napoleon had passed two nights in it. There was a prison to be seen, and several small rooms; and by-and-by they mounted to the roof. The old woman did not follow them there. They were alone. But each, for some reason, seemed to have grown shy of the other, and neither offered to resume the interrupted conversation. Instead of that they leaned over the battlements in silence; or if they spoke, it was only to comment on some trivial object.

At last Miss Capel said, 'See, in the distance there are mamma and the General coming. We had better go down and meet them. What is the use of our remaining here like this ?'

She spoke very softly; her voice was almost a whisper; and she moved towards the opening of the stair by which they had mounted.

'Let me go first,' said Carew, in a voice almost as low as her own. 'The steps are worn and slippery.'

He placed himself in the narrow doorway; his foot was on the first step: but there he paused and again looked at his companion, as if expecting some answer that had not yet been given him. She seemed to divine his thoughts, and to know that he still was dwelling on that one fact which he said he did understand about her; to know also that he was waiting for some answer. He saw, as he looked at her, that she was struggling to command her voice; but her eyes were like messengers, hurrying on before it. At last the voice came.

'Oh, why,' she said, 'do you talk about such things? It will not be for a long time. Why need we think about it now?'

The words and the look were full of a pleading sadness, and expressed a trust in him so complete and intimate, that it might have been called passionate had it not been so cloudless also. They were standing close together. Carew said nothing. He merely, as she spoke, drew her towards himself. She came unresistingly into the fold of his arms, and, bending down, he kissed her. Then they descended the stairs. In touching her lips he felt as if he had touched a flower.

During the drive home, sunk deep in a reverie, he kept asking himself, 'Was the flower a lotus or a forget-me-not ?'

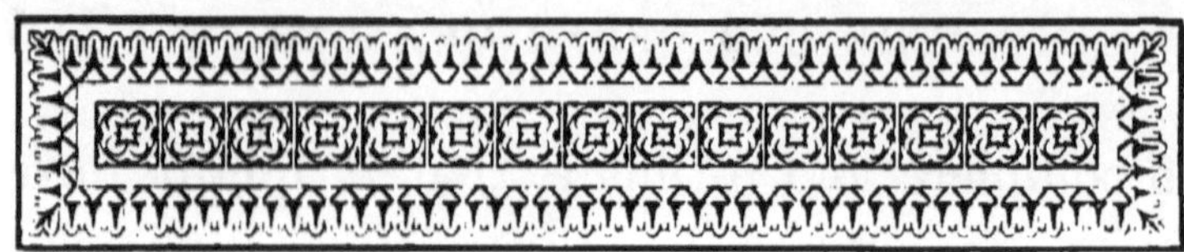

CHAPTER VIII.

ON their return that night, the General having duly left them, the little dinner of three had for all of them a peculiar charm :—not that the General was not missed ; he *was* missed : and the charm consisted precisely in the sense of intimacy, produced by the fact that they all had a loss in common. The homely evening that followed made the charm complete. Carew was surprised to find how all sorts of kindly thoughts, all sorts of small tastes and sympathies, which, so far as expression went, were usually frozen by his reserve, now began to declare themselves almost unintentionally, like drops of water from snows when they begin to thaw; and when the two ladies had gone to bed, he subsided again into his chair, and thought his situation over.

All that day, as if in a half-trance, he felt he had been drifting into a kind of fairyland. He remembered that in the morning there had been a few little far-off troubles ; but they had been over long ago. The touch of those lips that met his on the tower had been for him literally a kiss of peace ; and there had fallen on his mind the same sort of expectant calm that breathes and sleeps over a murmuring moonlit sea. He knew enough, however, of the ways of the heart's weather to know that such calms were often extremely treacherous. At present, he said to himself, he was in love delightfully. Was there any danger, he asked, of his becoming in love dangerously? And then he wavered, and asked was he really in love at all ? These questions, he found, were strangely pleasant to dwell upon ; and to clear his judgment about them, he went out into the moonlight.

The moonlight made the answers no more certain ; but there was an element of pleasure in their very uncertainty. He was certain of one thing only, and this was that whatever might be his relations to Miss Capel, her presence and influence made a magic circle round him, which kept, for the time at least, a world of troubles away from him. He felt that within that circle he had somehow grown years younger again. The desolating anxieties with which thought had made him familiar could not disappear, indeed, but they became semi-transparent phantoms. The voices of men asking in vain for spiritual guidance, the growth of democracy uneasily chafing for change, dwindled in his ears to a faint noise in a dream ; and the things close to him resumed their old reality. The crisp rustle of the palm fronds, the softer whispering of the orange-trees, the moonlight sleeping on the antique walls of the château, and the light from within that glowed at a certain window—these were the sights, these were the sounds which once more seemed to him to touch what is deeper in man's nature. Miss Capel was there above him, behind that lighted window; but her spirit, he felt, was everywhere. It glided in and out amongst the orange-trees; it was wandering below in the gardens; it floated up to him from the beds of violets. Was there danger in this—danger to him, to her? Was sorrow somehow lying in wait for either of them? The voice of the garden seemed to answer 'No!' and, breathing about his pillow as he softly sank to sleep, whispered that in love like this there was delight but no danger.

This comfortable but somewhat visionary

conclusion was hardly borne out by the next two days' experience. He did not, indeed, himself call it in question; but that was only because he was too much preoccupied to criticise it, and the hours flowed by in a stream of enchanted feeling, whose surface no obstacle fretted or troubled into thought. He discovered, it is true, during the course of the very next morning, when she resumed her work at his picture, that she not only distracted his mind from the subjects which used to absorb him, but that she could hardly herself understand what those subjects were. She knew as little of politics as if they were brewing or paper-making; and when, in allusion to the neighbouring room which he had shown her, he happened to say that he was interested in political economy, she repeated the two words with a soft contemptuous wonder, as if they meant to her as little as Mumbo Jumbo. This discovery he did reflect upon for a moment; for a moment it disappointed him; then he looked into her eyes and acquiesced in it. Nor was she, indeed, wanting in qualities by which this defect was atoned for. In poetry of the lyrical and more emotional kind she was exceedingly well read, and had a singularly sensitive appreciation of it; and in her own remarks on the emotional side of life not only was the same appreciation observable, but a certain shrewdness mixed with a dreamy pathos, which seemed to indicate that she had been at school under experience.

As to her engagement, as if by some tacit understanding, that was not again referred to; and as to their own affection, instinct taught both of them that they could indulge in it with the greatest ease by frankly and cheerfully ignoring it. By the morning after the picnic, the image of the Prince De Vaucluse, at least in Carew's mind, had receded into the background. It was lost amongst a multitude of other banished anxieties. Standing by the easel to watch how his portrait was progressing, he once more stooped down, and touched the lips of his flower. She raised her face to his, and to-day was joined to yesterday. The present closed about them like a cloud, hiding from them with a luminous mirage the hard world of consequences. They began to live and breathe together in a coloured cocoon of dreams.

Mrs. Capel, who was far from strong, and had been reminded of her weakness by the fatigue she felt after the picnic, was not inclined for any more active exercise than an occasional walk along the ramparts. Thus the two others, through all the sunshiny afternoons, roofed by the cloudless sky, and breathing the siren air, wandered about together, with no company but their own. The garden was a world for them, just as if they had been children. The banks, with their shrubs, seemed to rise to visionary altitudes. The blossoms of the camellia-trees seemed to touch the clouds. Sometimes, too, they carried their explorations farther. They strayed along the neighbouring hill-sides, amongst terraced vineyards and olive-groves. They threaded the peasants' footpaths ; they listened to the headlong brooks ; they plucked maidenhair from the crevices of wet rocks.

A day or two later, however, Miss Capel informed her mother that she had had a letter from some girl who had been at school with her. The contents of the letter, which she discussed in Carew's hearing, seemed to him trivial and indifferent enough ; but he noticed at the time a slight change in her manner—a slight sadness, a slight increase of thoughtfulness ; and by-and-by, when they were by themselves in the garden, this change, which in the interval he had thought might be only his fancy, again struck him, and struck him as unmistakable. She was sitting on a seat, under an arch of myrtle ; and he was standing a pace or two off, in front of her. Content and happy in the mere sense of her neighbourhood, he was not looking at her, but, with a lazy smile of amusement, was watching the movements of a long procession of caterpillars. Meanwhile her eyes had been fixed on him with a gentle persistence, as if nothing else were worth looking at. At last she pronounced his name ; and at once he turned towards her. Never before had her face been so full of meaning ; and never in her eyes, despite the smile that played in them, had there floated an expression of such sad alluring tenderness.

'Mr. Carew,' she said with a grave simplicity, 'I don't think I can ever let you go away from me.'

Carew had never in words made her a

direct declaration of any kind. She, indeed, had been far franker than he; and though she, like him, had said nothing about love, she had over and over again told him how much she liked him : but her perfect straight-forwardness, like perfect truth in a diplomat, had made him think she meant less than she said rather than more; and whilst adding to the piquancy of the situation had increased his sense of security in it. Now the case was different. Her words had something in them — he could not quite tell what —that thrilled him with a sense of their being really true. He paused for a moment, thinking what reply he should make to her. Words trembled on his lips almost as simple and straightforward as her own; but with an impulse whose source he had no time to analyze, he sharply repressed them, and only said regretfully, 'It is you who are going away from me, not I from

you.   But why do you talk of going away ?
You are not going yet ; and when you do—
well, perhaps I shall come with you.'

She looked round her at the garden and
all its flowers, as if she had not heard him.
' Don't you think,' she said absently, ' that all
this is very beautiful ? '   Carew replied that
he did.   ' I wonder,' she went on, ' whether
it would be equally beautiful if we were not
happy in it ?   I think its beauty to me is, that
it means my happiness.'

' And mine too,' said Carew. ' It means it,
it interprets it.   The light in those roses is
not only the sunshine.   It is the light of our
two lives, which they reflect back on us, with
some added light of their own.'

She suddenly began to murmur this verse
of Shelley's :

<blockquote>
' Like a glow-worm golden
In a dell of dew,
Scattering unbeholden
Its aërial hue.
</blockquote>

Do you think our lives in your garden have been like that ? Perhaps they have. Your garden will always have the same sunshine coming back to it, but never the same glow-worm. No, Mr. Carew,' she went on, trying to assume a tone of lightness, ' never, never, never the same glow-worm. Come,' she exclaimed, and she struggled still harder to command some tone of her ordinary conversational buoyancy, ' come—we've had enough poetry. It's tea-time, and I'm dying for my tea—tea, and some of that beautiful cake of yours. Cake !—Mr. Carew, doesn't it make your mouth water ? '

That evening the two ladies were somewhat late in coming down to dinner, and Carew was wondering what had possibly kept them, when Miss Capel entered the room, with a quicker step than usual, holding out and waving a small piece of blue paper. There was an odd brightness in her eyes, and she was humming an air of Offenbach's. 'Mr. Carew,' she exclaimed, stopping in the middle of a bar, 'didn't I say so—*never the same glow-worm* ?' And she laughed with an air that tried to seem one of gaiety.

Carew could do nothing but stare at her. She put the paper into his hand. It was a telegram from the General, and the purport of it was this : his wife's presence was needed at once at Genoa. 'To-morrow morning,' said Miss Capel, 'we must go to-morrow morning.' She raised her eyes, and the brightness had quite left them.

She had hardly done speaking when her mother entered, slightly agitated, and full of regrets and apologies. There was no cause whatever for any anxiety. Her presence at Genoa was simply needed to complete some legal formalities incident to the General's business, property of hers, as well as his being concerned in it ; but the necessity of leaving the château in this unexpected way discomposed her. Still it appeared that there was no help for it; she and her daughter must be off as early as might be, next morning, hoping in a very few days to come back with the General; and Miss Capel, having submitted to the inevitable, seemed only anxious to know if the post would come before they started.

Carew was able to satisfy her with an assurance that it would, wondering, as he did so, what this anxiety meant. Then, when the practical details of the departure had been settled, they fell to consoling themselves by making various plans for the happy time when they should all be reassembled.

In this way they passed a somewhat dejected evening. All their efforts were directed to dispelling a sense of sadness; but in spite of everything it still hung in the air. Then came the two 'good-nights'; the two ladies retired, and Carew was left alone in the drawing-room. A minute or two later the door opened softly, and Miss Capel came back again. At the sight of her an impulse seized him—an impulse which surprised himself—to rush forward and fold her in his arms, and say something—his impulse was rather vague as to what. But he mastered himself, and remained perfectly still; whilst a small voice, as of a prudential conscience, continued to whisper, ' One rash word, and you will commit yourself.'

She had come back for her work-basket. Carew rose to find it for her; but she saw it before he did, and, seizing it by a rapid movement, she was again at the door, as if she were afraid to linger. She paused there for a second, she cast one last glance at him, and, having lightly pressed her finger-tips to her lips, she was gone.

Carew once more sank back in his chair abstractedly. At last, with a distinctness which startled his own ears, he heard the following few words escape him: 'Marry her! I could as soon imagine myself marrying a fairy or a mermaid!'

By that time the following night she and her mother were at Genoa.

CHAPTER IX.

EEING that Carew, up to the last moment, could thus let prudence control and criticise impulse, it might be thought that he had been right in his estimate of his own situation, and that his devotion, whatever effect it might have produced upon Miss Capel, was certainly not strong enough to cause any great trouble to himself. And, indeed, until he was actually left alone, this continued to be his own view of the matter; but from that moment he began to see he was mistaken. He was like a man who has been drinking in a hot room for hours, and thinks he is quite sober till he finds himself in the fresh air. No sooner was his companion of the past week gone from him—no sooner had her carriage disappeared through the outer archway, than a solitude that might be felt took possession of his consciousness, and he began to understand gradually the real results of her company. Instead of passing away from him like a beautiful dream—a dream which was sure soon to return and continue itself, and which during its absence it was a pensive luxury to regret—she had taken half of his waking life away with her.

It was different some ten days back when Miss Consuelo Burton had left him, though he himself, for reasons far down in his mind, felt it a profanity to compare the two occasions. It was different then. Miss Consuelo Burton had some connection with his life, regarded as the life of a man with some high and rational purpose. When she had turned away from him, he felt as if he had been excommunicated. Now he felt merely as if he had been abandoned. He could connect Miss Capel with no purpose of any kind. He could reason about his longing for her as little as he could reason about thirst or hunger. He only felt she was gone and had left a blank behind her. He knew quite well that she had not gone willingly, and that there was also a prospect of her speedy return. But the mere fact of her absence quickly developed in his mind the same feeling of desertion he would have had if she had fled from him with a rival, and the same feeling of hopelessness he would have had if no return had been in question.

Whilst she was with him, enchanting as he felt her presence, he had never regarded her as any part of his own life. He had escaped, as it were, out of his own life into hers. He never imagined that he could take hers into his. He could form no picture of any practical career with her. Now the case was altogether reversed. He could form no picture of any practical career without her.

Her presence, he felt, would be more to him than gratified ambition, more than any sympathy on political or social matters, more than any successful struggle with the hated tendencies of the day; and to live for her, to guide her, to cherish her, to tend and defend this one single flower, would not indeed be more than duty—it would be duty itself.

During the day of her departure these thoughts and feelings developed rapidly like a fever, and his imagination by the evening was in a state of abnormal activity. Continually in the bright sunshine, and then again in the moonlight, he had looked down at the garden, with all its dells of flowers, thinking of her, in accordance with her own simile, as the glow-worm that had lit up everything with 'its aërial hue'; and before he could bring himself to attempt sleeping he was obliged to seek relief in beginning a passionate letter to her. This as he wrote it was a surprise, a revelation to himself. He was like a man whom a fever has literally taken possession of, and who starts on suddenly seeing his changed face in a glass.

'Everything,' he wrote, 'is blank to me now you are gone. Everything will be blank till you come back again. Shall I ever send these lines to you? I hardly know. I try to think I shall not, because then I shall feel bolder in speaking each thought as it shapes itself. Thoughts!—I am wrong; it is not thoughts that I desire to convey to you : it is simply a longing. And that longing—how shall I describe it? I cannot. It can be described no more than a perfume. It can be expressed only in a multitude of images, from which it seems to breathe, as the perfume breathes from the petal. As I am writing this the moonlight falls upon my paper, for the curtains are drawn back and my window is wide open. You, and my longing for you, are for my mind associated with that moonlight, and with the garden below me amongst whose odours it falls. Do you think I am talking nonsense ? It is nonsense unless you have the key to it. But you, on whom no shade of feeling is ever lost, you, my " glowworm golden in a dell of dew," perhaps you will understand me. Heart of my heart, life of my life, flesh of my flesh, spirit of my spirit, if I wake to-night I shall think all night of you. If I sleep, I shall dream of you.'

This was all he wrote ; and the following morning he shrank from re-reading it, much as he might have shrunk from touching some sensitive spot in his body. He did not fear that he had said more than he felt ; he feared seeing what he did feel too completely exposed. But a letter arrived for him by the post which sent all such scruples to the winds, and changed his fear that he had said too much into a contemptuous sense that he had said too little. The letter was dated Ventimiglia. He knew the handwriting. She had written to him so soon!

'We have nearly two hours,' Miss Capel began abruptly, ' to wait at this station ; so I seize the first opportunity of saying to you what must be said sooner or later. If one jumps out of bed in the morning the very moment one wakes, the act of getting up is easy. If one closes one's eyes again, one may struggle to rouse oneself for hours. The same is the case with the waking dreams of life. Years of trouble may be saved if one breaks away from them the first painful moment one realizes they have been only dreams.

'I have been dreaming. I don't know whether you have. Very possibly you have been only pretending to dream : indeed, now that my eyes are open, I can hardly venture to think it was otherwise. But what does that matter? I was not pretending ; and I am writing to you now very seriously to say that I must dream no more. I hope you do not think me rude. I hope I do not pain you. No—I don't think you will mind much ; but still this is abrupt and sudden, and you will wonder what is the meaning of it.

'Well, do you remember my last day, and a letter I got from an old school-friend of mine, in the morning? Mamma and I were talking about it. My friend, who is married, is a relation of the Prince de Vaucluse, and she wrote to say that she was going to send me a wedding present—a pair of earrings. That brought the reality of things back to me, though I tried not to think of it; and

 U

I might have put it away from me, if my friend had not said also that the Prince had come back to Paris. He has been at Southampton lately, where he keeps his yacht; and, now he was back in Paris, I knew I should at once hear from him. That was why I was so anxious about our letters yesterday when we were going away. I expected one from him; and I felt a kind of shyness in thinking that you might see it. It came. I had hoped—how wrong of me!— I had hoped it might be to say that his yacht was being got ready, and that he was going round the world in her. He meant to have done so : and that made what is going to happen seem so far off to me. And the letter really was to say he is coming to Nice—I think in three weeks; and in May we are to be married.

'It will be difficult for me to forget the days that I have passed with you; perhaps it will be impossible. But I must do my best to forget them, or never to think of them with any kind of tenderness. No, Mr. Carew; there must be no half measures for me. If I had my own way, I would not even come back to Courbon-Loubet, as mamma and the General propose doing. But it would be very difficult for me to remain away; and I have not the courage, the determination, to face the difficulty. Else I couldn't ever look at you again—not till I could do so without remembering. Will that time ever come?

'We shall be at the Hôtel de Gênes. Will you write me a line there? When we meet again everything will be so very different; and a few kind words from you would make things a little easier.'

Then followed the signature. It was simply 'Violet.'

This letter had a singular effect upon Carew. His fever in reading it passed rapidly into an acuter phase; and the thought that

Miss Capel seemed on the point of escaping him did much to ripen a definite wish to seize her. Life if he lost her, he felt, would have no taste in it. He turned to the letter he had himself begun last night. All shyness of his own protestations had left him ; and in their strained excited language he now found a futile comfort. He tore the paper up, however, for two reasons. Its language was not strained and not excited enough ; and there was also no answer in it to the news he had received this morning. He began writing afresh to her, and in a more vehement way. What he had said before he repeated with added emphasis, and there ran through his phrases what in his first letter was wanting— a note of pain and decision, that gave them a certain *brusquerie.*

' You speak,' he wrote in conclusion, ' you speak of your dream ending. Why must you end it ? What constraint is put upon you ? Consider how young you are, how your whole life is before you. It has seemed to me that that life of yours has just begun to unfold itself, petal by petal, trembling to the light. And now, if you do what you talk of doing, there will be nothing in store for you but blight and darkness. The rose tree of your life will live, but the rose will be gone. There will be no second blossoming. Have the courage to continue dreaming, and the dream will become the reality. Do you doubt that ? Let me tell you one thing. To me what were once realities have become dreams; and the dream which you and I have dreamt together has become the one, the only reality. I will ask this of you. Decide on nothing till you return here. Let us meet, for a few days at least, as we have met before. Those days may be the earnest of a happy future ; or they will be something —a small something—saved from a dark one.'

It occurred to him after he had sent this letter off that even now he had made no direct and practical proposal to her. There had been much mention of dreams; and he thought he must have seemed like a lover literally pleading in dreamland—a land where there was no marrying and no marriage settlements. Mere emotion, however, possessed him far too completely to allow much foothold in his mind for critical reflections such as this; and until an answer came from her he hardly knew what to do with himself. One thing he did know—he could not remain quiet; and when he entered the study where he had once been so absorbed and industrious, and looked at his shelves of Ricardo, Marx, and Bastiat, they affected his mind with the same sort of repulsion that a man about to be sea-sick feels for a leg of mutton.

At last the letter he had been so longing

for came. The beginning of it piqued him by its coldness ; but he saw in a moment or two that the coldness was artificial ; and the ending touched him in a quite unexpected way.

'I had hoped,' she said, ' that in waking up from my dream I should, indeed, have found one part of it a reality. I dared to hope so ; and the part I speak of was your friendship. I had hoped you would help me. I am quite alone in the world. It is very hard to do right. Am I preferring a very presumptuous request when I ask you not to make. it harder—as you so easily, so very easily can ? '

He had been utterly unprepared for any appeal of this kind. He had pictured her suffering from many an emotional struggle, but never from a moral one. Just as she had seemed a stranger to his political and his social anxieties, so had he conceived of her as a

stranger to the conflict between virtue and
wrong-doing. The idea of vice he had never
for a moment associated with her ; but he
had as little associated with her the idea of
virtue. In the singular quality of her ingenu-
ousness she had seemed like Eve before the
fruit of the tree of knowledge had been eaten ;
and the only standard she had suggested to
him hitherto had been that of her refined
and easily wounded feelings, and her seeming
need of some deep and unfound affection.
He recalled her volume of poems that dealt
with spiritual subjects, and the lines at the
beginning of it that had been addressed to
herself; but all that had seemed to perplex
rather than appeal to her. He recalled, too,
the incident of her having stolen off to church
alone ; but even then she seemed to have
acted not so much like a devotee as like a
child, or a stray dog looking for some friend.

Now he saw his error, though he could

not fully realize it ; and too late his conscience began to smite him, not only for the hasty and false judgment he had formed of her, but for the way in which by her undefended affections he had led her into sorrow and danger.

> It's dangerous work to play with souls,
> And matter enough to save one's own—

these lines of Robert Browning's kept on constantly recurring to him ; and the thought expressed in them, with the personal reproach implied in it, mixed in his mind with a feeling for her of contrite pity. He wrote, in answer to her, a subdued and gentle letter, promising to give her whatever help he could.

'It seems hard,' he said, ' that in this case my truest sympathy for you must be shown by suppressing nearly every sign of itself ; and that the help you speak of must consist in holding out no hand to you. But if it must be so it must. The bitterest reproach you could ever bring against me would be, that I had caused you to reproach yourself.'

He thought that in thus writing he was saying farewell to all his former relations with her; but in this very act of renouncing his affection, that affection deepened. It took a new glow and colour, as suddenly as some cloud does in the sunrise; and having seized his pen again, he added this postscript: 'When you come, I shall ask you a definite question, and you must be prepared to answer it one way or another. Is not some change in your plans possible?'

He looked at the words for some moments reflectively; and at last, acting under a vague combination of motives, he tore up the separate sheet they were written on.

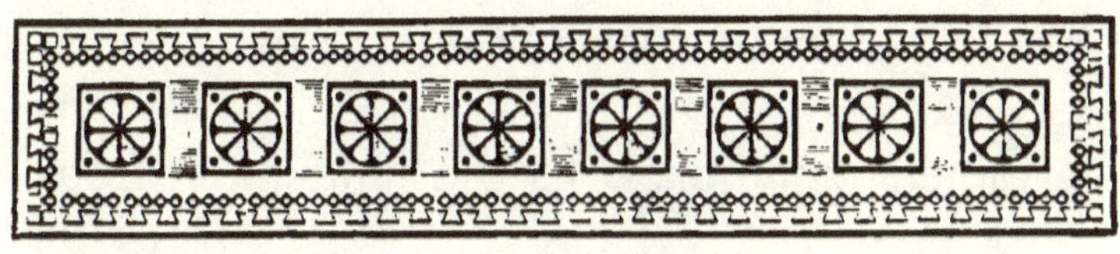

CHAPTER X.

WHEN two friends quarrel through the medium of correspondence, and without seeing each other, the estrangement is apt to seem far greater than it really is, or than, if they had met, it would have seemed to be. The same is true of every difference of feeling which takes place under the same circumstances : and when a meeting does take place at last, there is a surprise on either side at the sight of the familiar features, instead of the far-off phantasmal face that had seemed to stare coldly through the letter-paper.

Carew was keenly conscious of this when

the Capels came back to the château. Looking at Miss Capel as she sat opposite him at
dinner, noting in her eyes exactly the same
softness and the same sparkle that seemed to
leap with pleasure at the sight of him, he
could hardly believe that this was really the
person who had been begging, almost order-
ing, him to keep a chilly distance from her.
One thing only reminded him that such was
the case ; and this was the way in which she
treated a piece of intelligence that was for
him exceedingly disappointing. His visitors
could not possibly remain more than two
nights with him. The day after to-morrow
they were obliged to go back to Cannes ; and
Miss Capel in a number of ways, imperceptible to anyone but himself, gave him to understand that this plan had her entire approbation. She declared that Cannes was the
loveliest place in the world ; that nothing
was pleasanter than to drink chocolate, with

delicious whipped cream at a certain con·
fectioner's on the Promenade ; and she asked
Carew what he would advise her to wear at a
ball which next week would be given at the
Cercle Nautique.

After dinner he tried to speak to her alone,
as she used to be giving him occasions to do
constantly. But she avoided any incident
of this kind with a tact so extraordinary
that he could hardly tell whether the avoid-
ance were not unintentional. The only sign
which convinced him it was not so was a sort
of mischievous triumph which he detected
once or twice in her eyes. For the rest, her
behaviour was superficially quite the same to
him ; she talked, laughed, sang, just as she
had done. But in spite of this he felt that
everything was changed ; and he went to bed
with a sense of provocation and bitterness
which he could not appease, though he knew
it was wholly unjustified.

The following morning he fancied himself more lucky. He had thought she was sitting with her mother in the large saloon, and having gone for a book into a small sitting-room next to it, he was surprised and delighted at finding her there alone. But the moment he approached her she seemed to shrink away from him, something like a bird which, although perfectly tame, betrays a horror of having a hand laid on its feathers. He sat down on a chair close to her, and said, in a forced voice, 'My picture is not finished yet.'

A book lay in her lap. She looked down at it, and began turning over the pages.

'No,' she said, 'that must wait till some other time.'

'*It* is not finished,' exclaimed Carew, 'but something else is.'

'What else ?'

Carew paused for a moment, and then

said, almost fiercely, 'What you call a dream, and what I call a reality.'

She appeared to take no notice of this, but merely turned over the pages rather quicker than before; then, springing from her seat, she said, 'This is the wrong volume; I must go and fetch the other,' and she moved lightly towards the door of the large saloon.

But Carew was there before her, and, with his hand on the handle, confronted her with a gaze of inquiry.

'Mr. Carew, will you let me go by?' she said. 'Please — please — I am in a hurry.'

And she tried to give to her voice an air of petulant playfulness.

'In one moment,' he said, 'in one moment. But first—I may never be alone with you again—first say good-bye to me.'

'Do you want to get rid of us yet?' she

said. 'I thought you were going to have kept us as your guests till to-morrow.'

'It is you,' he retorted, 'who are anxious to get rid of me. You have already driven me to the door of your heart. Well, won't you say good-bye to me before the door is slammed?'

He took her hand, which she surrendered to him passively.

'Will you,' he murmured, 'not kiss me once more?'

He leaned towards her, but as he did so she drew back.

'No, Mr. Carew,' she answered, 'never, never again.'

And she looked at him, not with anger exactly, but with a little pout of refusal. She seemed almost as childlike in her resistance to temptation as she had been in her forgetfulness that such a thing as temptation existed.

'Why,' she exclaimed, half teasingly, half sadly, 'why do you look so cross? Mr. Carew, will you pick that letter up for me?'

He stooped to do so. In a moment she was half through the door, and, receiving the letter with a parting smile, she disappeared.

'Mamma,' she said, an hour or two later, when, having fetched her work, she was seated beside her mother, 'where is Mr. Carew? We have not seen him for some time.'

'Didn't you hear what he told me?' said Mrs. Capel. 'You must have been out of the room, then. He has had some business in the neighbourhood which has called him away, and it is very possible that he will not be back till the evening.'

Miss Capel changed colour suddenly. She became first white, then she flushed scarlet.

'And we,' she said presently, 'go early to-morrow!'

Nothing more was seen of Carew for hours. He re-entered the saloon a little after five, and found Mrs. Capel, who had finished her tea, just quitting it.

'Well,' he exclaimed, with an air as careless as he could command, 'I've done my business. I've had a hard day's work of it. I have been as far as Beaulieu.'

Mrs. Capel turned back for a moment. She asked if he was not thirsty, and said the tea was still quite warm.

'I shall be down again in a moment,' she added. 'Violet will pour you out a cup. See how I am doing the honours in your own house!'

He had not at first noticed Miss Capel; but there she was, in a low chair by the tea-table. She looked up at him, and the flush came again into her cheeks.

'You have been at Beaulieu?' she said.

'On business—yes,' he replied coldly, still standing at a distance from her, and making no offer to advance.

'Come,' she said, 'will you not have your tea?'

'Will you allow me,' he said in a strained changed voice, 'to come near you? I hardly know on what I may venture.'

'Come,' she repeated, and this time so gently that he moved forward and took a seat close to her. 'Mr. Carew, how can you talk in that way? Why do you? And so you have been to Beaulieu—and on business? What business?'

'Shall I tell you?' said Carew. 'To avoid any chance of giving pain to you as you are now, and to live over once more an hour with you as you were then. I rode there. I rode as hard as I could. I put my horse up at the hotel, and I walked on to the promontory—our promontory. Perhaps you have forgotten it.'

' It would be well for me,' she said, in a choked tone, ' if I had.'

' And I sat there, on a rock,' he continued, ' looking at our tower, shining in to-day's sunlight just as it did in yesterday's. I couldn't go near it—I hadn't the heart for that. I found—do you know what I found? It was the fragments of one of our wine-bottles, which you had broken against a stone. My life was lying at the foot of that tower, broken into pieces by you, just as you broke that bottle. Whilst I was sitting there I wrote something I want to show you. Will you look at it? '

He held out to her a piece of paper with something in pencil scribbled on it. Whilst she was reading he watched her, his chin resting on his hand. What she deciphered was this. It was headed ' The

Tower at Beaulieu;' and then came what follows :

One true hour of love lies there,
Dead in the clear unburying air.
Hear distracted Memory call,
' Who shall give it burial?'
Memory! thou of little wit,
There be three shall bury it.
Let the World, false, vain, and loud,
Be the grave-clothes and the shroud;
Let the Devil's Scorn of Good
Be the heavy coffin-wood;
And let false love be the clay
That hides all from the light of day.

She was a long time bending over the paper. She must have read the lines several times, and once or twice he saw that she bit her lip. At last she raised her eyes, and two large tears fell from them. She held her hand out to him ; he took it ; she pressed his convulsively, and then abruptly dropped it.

'You mustn't,' she murmured, 'be angry with me. You must be always my friend. By-and-by I shall want friends more than ever. Listen!' she exclaimed, starting slightly, and making a strong effort to recover her natural manner, 'I hear mamma coming. She is gone into the next room—yes, I know why. She has gone to see if I have left any of my goods about. Let us go to her. Do be civil to her. Don't let her imagine that you are thinking of other things. Did you hear what I just said ? What will your opinion of the Capel family be ? Mamma does the honours of your own house to you, and I give you lessons in how to do the honours yourself.'

Whilst she was speaking she had risen, and a smile had at length come back to her. She was looking down at him, motioning him to rise also ; and in that downward smile there seemed to him to be something compassionate, as if, despite all that was childlike in her, she knew more of life than he did. He rose. As he did so her smile grew tenderer, and, putting her hand on his shoulder, she quickly and softly kissed him. But how different was the touch of her lips now to what it had been on the tower ! It was nothing now but a sign of pity and concession. It was he who was like a child now—a poor refractory child—and her kiss was like a sugarplum given to him at last furtively and under protest. This was his last private interview with her before she left the château.

CHAPTER XI.

HEN the Capels departed, the following morning, both the General and his wife said many civil things about their hopes that Carew would come often to Cannes and see them. Miss Capel also murmured something to the same effect, but she did so mechanically, putting little or no meaning into it. She was leaving him thus ! He could hardly bear the thought. He determined that he would not wait long before he came to some better understanding with her, and, just as the carriage was beginning to move off, he called after it to her, ' I shall be at Cannes the day after to-morrow.' She looked round, waved her hand to him, and he could just catch the words, 'Certainly; we shall expect you.'

During the last few days his mind had been so much occupied that he had allowed an accumulation of business letters to remain unanswered, some of them even unopened. He resolved now to kill the day in attending to them. When, however, he was sitting down at his writing-table, the first thing that caught his eye was a little three-cornered note placed conspicuously upon his blotting-book. It was from Miss Capel. It ran thus:

'I am writing good-bye to you, for I do not know how to say it. I am afraid you must think me a very odd person. This is partly due to circumstances which I cannot explain, and partly to another cause, which I could explain if it would not make you angry. You do not now think enough of the position in which I stand. If you did, you would see that I am not different, but that I am obliged to seem different—and not only now, but for always. Would you wish it to be otherwise? I thought you were going to help me, and not make things harder for me. I have heard again from *him*. He is coming to Cannes a fortnight hence, perhaps, and then everything may happen much sooner than was at first intended. It all seems so strange, I can hardly realize it. We shall see you again soon. I shall like that. Like it ! You see the language I am obliged to use to you. It is like withered roses.

'When you meet me I must leave it to you to settle with your own conscience how you will behave to me. Good-bye. God bless you. I hardly know what I am writing. There are some feelings, Mr. Carew, which we must bury, even though they may not be dead.'

Carew's business letters at once went out

of his head. Having read Miss Capel's note several times over, he slowly took from a drawer some crumpled sheets of paper, scribbled with pencil jottings ; and, spreading these before him, pressed his head on his hands and began poring over them. By-and-by he began writing, not continuously, but at irregular intervals. After his luncheon he took a short walk, and then returned again to this same occupation. What its nature was will be seen from the following letter, which he enclosed that night in an envelope directed to Miss Capel.

' You tell me to consult my conscience as to how I ought to meet you again. I have consulted my conscience, and I hardly know what it says. You think your position must be clear to me. I answer you it is not so. You are engaged to marry a man you do not care for, and with whom you do not sympathize. You do sympathize with me.

Why must this marriage take place ? Surely you are a free agent. There is no constraint put upon you.

'Put me for one moment out of your head entirely, and think of me as pleading not for my sake but for your own. It is better, far better, not to marry at all than to marry as you propose to do. Be wise in time. It will be too late soon. I can think of no fate more terrible, more ruinous, for you than to be tied to a man who is wholly unable to sympathize with you; and you know as well as I do that such is the man in question.

'But, Violet, my own Violet, let me suppose the worst. Let me suppose that a promise binds you, which, for some reason unknown to me, you must fulfil at all costs. I will suppose it does. Well—what then ? I have still one prayer to make to you. When the time comes you will marry him—you will redeem your promise—you will be true to it on the reckoning day. But what meanwhile ? Listen.

'Just as a promise will claim you then, meanwhile an affection claims you. Need you be in such haste to show yourself false to *it*—to it which claims, and can claim you for such a little while longer ? If for that little while you continue to be to me all you have been, we shall be but seeing our last of what we both realize we must part with. It would be very different if we renewed our friendship afterwards. We should then be plunging into danger, not saying good-bye to happiness. Violet, for your sake I would never allow that.

'I fear myself to speak of that time; I hardly dare look forward to it. How could I ever endure to see you pass me in the street, under those altered circumstances ? Could I endure to see that face that has been

so often near mine, far—far away from me ?
—those lips that have so often kissed me, open
to me only in some chilly commonplace, or
with a cordiality far colder than coldness ?
Violet, everything here recalls you to me—
the gardens, the ramparts, the little chair
you oftenest sat in, and every distant mountain whose shadows we have watched changing : but most of all Beaulieu, and the old
tower there.   All that afternoon which I
spent there by myself, when you drove me
away, words, expressions, thoughts, came
thronging into my brain and clustering
into—I won't call it poetry—but metrical
expression.   I had not to hunt for rhymes
and phrases, but merely to choose from the
crowd that swarmed round me, soliciting me
like beggars : and they had all to do with
you. To-day I have been trying to make
them intelligible, thinking I would send
them to you.   Then I thought they would

strike you as unreal and artificial ; and I began this common letter to you instead. But they are not artificial. They may be bad poetry ; but, Violet—what name shall I call you that will express my longing for you ?—they show what I mean, what I am, far better than this prose does. I didn't call them, they came to me. Remember this as you read them. You will see that all you urge in that little note of yours filled my mind yesterday as I wandered alone at Beaulieu.

Which is the better, which the kinder part—
   To leave you quite, to cast you quite aside,
And in one cold farewell to hide with art
   The pain and passion nature will not hide ;
Or, still to hold and fold you to my heart,
   And, in a vain dream, dream you still my bride,
Nor ever call one loving word the last,
Until the past become indeed the past?

This is the question which, the whole blank day,
   I ask my heart as I sit here alone,
Watching the dull waves break in Beaulieu bay ;
   And answer from my heart receive I none.

What makes it mute? you ask.   I will not play
　　With hackneyed phrases.   Oh, my own, my own,
There is no need to say my heart is breaking;
Pain makes it mute, although 'tis only aching.

Pain in my heart, and silence in my ears,
　　Gloom in my eyes—my eyes and ears that miss
Your eyes and voice, and vague regrets and fears
　　Clouding my thoughts—my life is come to this:
With one keen sense through all, that all my years
　　Have closed their meaning in your hopeless kiss.
Ah! once again, before the moment slips,
Love, let me leave my life upon your lips.

What! do you chide me for that desperate cry,
　　And say I tempt you?   Yes, I feel you do.
Listen to me, then; I have this reply:
　　Let Love, my loved one, judge 'twixt me and you.
Inquire of Love, who still stands lingering by,
　　And gives us still his licence to be true,
And will not wholly leave us, till betwixt
My life and yours there is the great gulf fixed.

Ask Him, for He has made you one with me;
　　You are with me, and around me everywhere.
I feel you in the mountains and the sea,
　　And when I breathe you feed me in the air.
And oh, my soul's true soul, the thought of thee
　　Moves me to pray, and mixes with my prayer.
Ask Him, for still—He still can point to-day
Towards Heaven, and say, 'In me behold the way.'

> Ask Him to-day.   He will have said ' Farewell,'
>   Farewell to you, farewell to me—to-morrow :
> And where He dwelt another Love will dwell,
>   With haggard, pitying eyes, and lips that borrow
> Their hopeless sentence from the gates of Hell,
>   ' Through me the way is to the eternal sorrow ' ;
> And lure and warn us in the same low breath—
> ' Take life from me, but know my life is death.'

' Remember what I have said. When your fate is settled, I will never allow myself to see you again. I will not run the risk of guiding you to the eternal sorrow. Now, and now only, is the accepted time. You may be to me as you have been for a few days longer : you may, if you will, be everything to me, for all your life. But you know the condition. It is that you free yourself from your present engagement.'

Carew's business letters received no attention that day. The following morning he had a note from Mrs. Capel, saying, ' Come to us to-morrow as early as you can. We propose to give *you* a little picnic in return

for the one you gave us; and we think of
going to a place amongst the Esterel mountains, not far from Théoule. Be with us, if
you can, by twelve.'

This arrangement delighted him, and he
at once wrote to acquiesce in it. Then, in
somewhat better heart, he addressed himself
to the pile of documents which he had too
long neglected, and he soon found one of
them to be of quite unexpected interest.

Its perusal produced one instant effect.
He hastily tore up the letter which he had
written to Mrs. Capel, and substituted
another for it in which, while accepting the
invitation, he said he should be unable to
meet them at Cannes. He would, instead,
go to Théoulé by train, and wait for them
there at the railway station, which they
would naturally pass in driving.

CHAPTER XII.

'HERE he is ! I can see him through the railings ! ' This was Miss Capel's exclamation. Her eyes were quicker than her parents. ' He is on the platform, standing by an enormous pile of luggage. Who with so much luggage can have possibly got out at Théoule, I wonder ? '

The Capels' carriage drew up at the little wayside station ; and Carew, after a few moments' conversation with one of the officials, came out through the wicket, and they were presently proceeding on their journey.

He now had time to look at the girl's face.   He at once noticed that the tint in her cheeks had faded.   The light still gleamed in her eyes, but it was not so buoyant as usual, and, for the first time during his whole acquaintance with her, her childlike and fearless frankness had given place to a certain timidity.   As, however, she watched Carew's behaviour, her old manner, little by little, returned to her.   She had anticipated that his attention or his reproachful silence might embarrass her, but she was surprised and relieved at finding that nothing of this kind happened ;   and that, instead, he appeared to be distracted by some quite alien subject. She was relieved, but she was slightly piqued ; and, under the influence of the latter feeling, she began to attack him with a little volley of questions.   Why had he not joined them at Cannes and driven with them ?   What had he done with himself since they left ? What was he talking about so confidentially to the man at the station ? Who had got out of the train with that imposing pile of luggage ? To the last question alone did she get any definite answer.

'The luggage,' Carew said, ' is mine.'

Her cheeks flushed with pleasure ; and yet from her eyes there came a moment's glance of reproach.

'What ! ' she exclaimed, ' and are you really coming to stay at Cannes for a little ? '

' At Cannes ? ' he repeated. ' No. I am on my way back to England.'

Mrs. Capel and the General were loud in their expressions of regret ; but Miss Capel did not utter a word.

' Family matters,' said Carew, ' have re-called me suddenly. Before long I hope to be back in the South again ; though circumstances,' and here he looked towards Miss Capel, 'may be such as to make me exchange Courbon-Loubet for Italy. Our picnic the other day ended with our seeing off the General to Genoa. To-day you must return the compliment, and see me off from Théoule station to London.'

The picnic was pleasant and uneventful enough, having nothing special to mark it, excepting the beauty of the scene—an open spot in the folds of a pine-clad valley. Carew and Miss Capel both did their best to exhibit the signs of an ordinary cheerful friendship, and hopes were expressed both by him and all the others that, in the course of a fortnight or so, he would be once more among them. As soon, however, as the last biscuit had been eaten, and the inevitable cigar-case was emerging from the General's pocket, Miss Capel said, with a soft, imperious laugh, ' I'm not going to let Mr. Carew stop smoking here with papa. I'm going to take him with me for one last walk along the valley. You know the path, mamma. It is the way we went last year.' Miss Capel was evidently accustomed to have her way in everything —at all events in matters of this description; and she and Carew were soon going together through a narrow forest path, with brushwood on each side of them. For some time they said very little, and what they did say was mere constrained trivialities. At last, after a pause of unusual length, Miss Capel began thus :

'And so, Mr. Carew, you are really going away, are you?'

'I am,' said Carew drily.

'And this time to-morrow,' she went on, 'you will be—how far away?—a thousand miles, at least.'

'You,' said Carew, 'are going farther away from me than I voluntarily should ever go from you. You can come to England—the place to which I am going; but you are going to a place to which I can never follow you.'

'Why not?' she said. 'You may be my friend still. So far as our friendship goes there need be no difference.'

'You are talking nonsense!' he retorted angrily. 'So far as our friendship goes, there must be every difference. If you wish,' he went on presently, 'that I should put the matter in plain words to you, I will do so. I love you far too well to see you only as a friend; and under the circumstances, which you are deliberately choosing for yourself, I love you far too well to dream of your being more than a friend. So there is nothing left us, you see, but to say a long good-bye; and if possible to think no more about it.'

'Exactly,' she said, 'that is just what you

will do, Mr. Carew. I know you better than you know yourself. I do not say you will think no more about it, but you will certainly think very little. You will think a little; —yes, I believe you will do that.' Carew was about to open his lips in protest. 'No,' she said, 'don't look hurt or angry. You think you are fond of me. You think I am necessary to your happiness. But what charms you is not me. It is the echoes in your heart which I have chanced to awaken—the echoes which go on wandering from dell to dell, and the birds there I have awaked also. It is all in yourself. There is very little music in me. I don't complain. I am simply telling you what is. Very soon you will have no regret for me. I shall be a pleasant memory you will not shrink from looking back upon. As for me, I shall wish that I had never met you.'

'You are wrong,' he said, 'why should

you think that?' But he spoke in a voice which hardly asked for an answer.

At the same moment the path took a turn which brought them, on a sudden, in full view of the sea. She seemed glad of an excuse to change the subject.

'There,' she said, 'is the view I wished to show you.'

He too seemed equally glad to escape to any triviality, even to the fact of his being, as she spoke, caught in a dangling bramble.

'Look,' he said, 'you have landed me in the thorns of life already. I am caught completely, and all owing to the path by which you have taken me.'

'It is hitched in your coat,' she said, 'just behind your collar. Let me pull it off for you.'

She stepped up on the bank at one side of the path, and she thus stood looking down on him from a vantage-ground of a few inches. She seized both ends of the bramble and began to free it from him ; but suddenly her purpose changed : she gently drew it round him, more closely than before, and watched him as she held him there bound in this mimic fetter. At last she said :

'I have possession of you now. I don't think that I shall ever let you go again.'

'Don't,' he said gravely. 'Keep me— keep me always. It is what I ask you to do.'

'Tell me,' she said, 'shall I come with you this afternoon to England ? I won't let you go till you tell me that.'

But Carew made no immediate answer. They both spoke as if they were tantalizing themselves with ideas rather than proposing possibilities. At last Carew said, in a constrained and painful voice :

'I have no home in England to which I could take you—at all events I do not know if I have. Many things have happened since last I saw you ; or, rather, I should say, I have learnt many things. My future is in my own hands no more than yours is—perhaps not so much.'

'Mine,' she said absently, 'is not in my own hands at all.' And then, as if her thoughts were straying still farther, she began to murmur something to herself in an indistinct monotone.

'What are you saying ?' he asked her.

She stopped, and looked at him with a faint momentary smile. 'Something,' she said, 'that I was reading over yesterday —verses, Mr. Carew, verses. I found them in a collection of Dramatic Lyrics, arranged and selected by the author, Mr. Robert Browning.'

'Tell me them,' said Carew. 'What were they ?'

She seemed to hesitate between seriousness and a forced air of mockery. In a moment or two she was serious; and in a tone something like that of a child learning to recite a prayer—except that in this case there was deep emotion veiled by it—she began to recite, gravely fixing her eyes on him :

'It all comes to the same thing in the end,
    Since mine thou art, mine wast, and mine shalt be,
Faithful or faithless, sealing up the sum,
Or lavish of thy treasure, thou must come
    Back to the heart's place which I keep for thee.'

As she finished, by an impulse that seemed instinctive, she began to extend her arms, as if inviting him to come to her; and at last she murmured almost below her breath :

' Say good-bye to me ! '

But the moment he moved a step nearer to her, her purpose abruptly changed; and lightly descending from the bank on which she was still standing, she began to walk at a rapid pace back towards the scene of the picnic.   Carew followed her with a sense of complete bewilderment, which was not lessened by the fact that when she looked behind her for an instant she seemed to be once more smiling.   He called to her to stop ; he asked her where she was going ; then he quickened his pace.   No sooner, however, did she find him coming up to her than she suddenly took to running, saying, in a voice that suggested laughter and tears equally :

'Run, Mr. Carew, run !   Can't you see— I am racing you.'

To this invitation he made no response. On the contrary, he began to walk more slowly again ; and watched her glancing figure as it sped away from him.   When, however, she was about a hundred yards ahead of him, she stopped short, and turned round, waiting for him.

'Come, Mr. Carew,' she exclaimed, as soon as he was within speaking distance; 'here are Mamma and the General. They have been making tea for you, and you are to have some before you begin your journey.'

And a moment afterwards the two elders appeared.

'It's a cruel kindness,' said the General, 'not to speed the parting guest, if he must part, however sorry we may be to lose him. But from what you say about your train, you have not too much time, if we intend to do things comfortably.'

They returned together to the spot where they had had their luncheon. They drank their tea; and in spite of efforts at gaiety, there were signs of sadness apparent in all the party. Still more was this the case when they again entered the carriage, and the horses' heads were directed towards the station.

'When do you get to Paris?' 'When do you get to Calais?' 'So far as we can judge, you will have an excellent passage'—such were the remarks and questions which, with the inevitable answers, did duty for conversation during Carew's last twenty minutes with his friends; and even this was kept up with difficulty, for, towards the end, Miss Capel became wholly silent; nor did she even raise her eyes till Carew had actually descended, and then he saw that they were tremulous with tears, which, as all her face showed, she was struggling not to shed.

Ten minutes later he was leaning back in the railway carriage, partly occupied with the perplexities of his immediate future, partly with the scenes that were drifting away behind him.

And it was thus they had said good-bye, so he bitterly told himself, with no explanation either on the one side or the other. Then he thought of the cause that was taking him back to England, and exclaimed wearily, 'I was right. It was best that I did not speak.'

END OF THE SECOND VOLUME.

G. & C.
PRINTED BY
SPOTTISWOODE AND CO., NEW-STREET SQUARE
LONDON